TOP HAND

TOP HAND

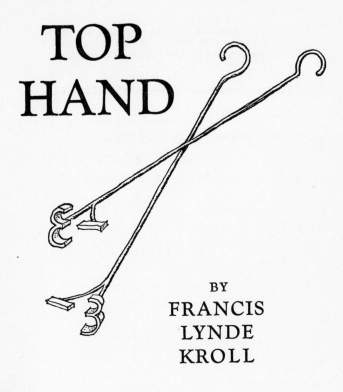

BY
FRANCIS
LYNDE
KROLL

decorations by Raymond Abel

DAVID McKAY COMPANY, Inc.   NEW YORK

TOP HAND

MANUFACTURED IN THE UNITED STATES OF AMERICA

VAN REES PRESS

Typography by Charles M. Todd

To VIOLA
*whose help
and encouragement
have made this story possible*

TOP HAND

1

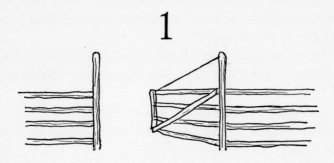

Bᴇʀᴛ Wᴇsᴛᴏɴ covered the pancakes on his plate with generous slabs of butter and then drowned both pancakes and butter in golden honey. Before he took the first bite, he looked up at his grandfather. A smile lit up his freckled face.

"Gramp," he said, "you make the best pancakes in the world."

Gramp turned from the stove where he was filling another plate. There was an answering smile on his face.

"You don't have to flatter me to get a day off." He chuckled. "We'll go to town and get a load of block salt."

"It wasn't flattery," Bert protested as soon as he had swallowed and was able to talk. "Anyway, I don't want to go to town today. I'd rather stay home and ride that south fence. I don't want Mr. Henderson coming over here to complain about his cattle getting through."

"I don't know why he should complain. It's our hay his cattle will eat if they get through the fence."

1

"He'll complain anyway," Bert insisted.

"Let him complain." Gramp snorted. "We'll ride that fence tomorrow. A fourteen-year-old boy is entitled to an occasional trip to town."

"In a few weeks high school will be starting and then I'll be going to town every day," Bert pointed out. "I'll take care of the fence today."

"All right," Gramp agreed reluctantly.

Bert reached for his hat. "I'll feed the horses so I can get started," he said before going out.

His dog Spot was waiting for him. Spot looked considerably like a collie, although his hair was shorter and his nose less pointed than that of most collies. A patch of dark hair around his left eye had earned him his name.

Spot scampered excitedly around the yard as Bert walked to the gate, opened it, stepped through, and quickly swung it shut. The dog stopped his scampering and dashed toward the gate as if he would jump over it. Instead, he stopped and watched Bert wistfully. Bert went on toward the barn as though he had completely forgotten the dog. Suddenly he stopped and turned.

"Come on, Spot," he called.

Spot sailed over the gate and dashed to Bert's side. He paused long enough to let the boy pet him before he raced off, running in great circles. When Bert came near the barn door, Spot stopped his dashing around and walked quietly at his master's heels.

"Wait here," Bert ordered as he went into the barn.

Obediently Spot crouched outside the door. Bert tossed hay into the mangers for the two horses. He took grain from the bin, poured it into the feed boxes and watched the horses begin to eat. After a few minutes he got a saddle from the rack and tossed it on the older of the two.

"Steady, Blaze," he called softly as he reached under and caught the dangling girth to pull it tight.

While he waited for Blaze to finish his grain, Bert went to the tool shed for the equipment he would need. He filled his pockets with staples and took a short length of barbed wire in case he must splice broken wires. His hammer wasn't in its accustomed place. He searched for it until he remembered he had left it on the porch. Back to the house he went, Spot trotting at his heels. Gramp was standing in the doorway, watching.

"I'm still afraid Spot will cause trouble," he said.

"Oh, no," Bert protested. "He minds too well for that. He'll never run off with a pack of wild dogs."

"I hope not." Gramp sounded doubtful.

Bert knew Gramp was remembering the pack of wild dogs that had done much harm in the neighborhood two years ago. The dogs had killed so many calves and caused so many stampedes that the ranchers had finally organized a hunt to be rid of them. The county officials, urged on by the Ranchers' Protective Association, had passed severe rules about stray dogs. Any rancher now had the right to shoot a dog that wandered onto his ranch. But Bert wasn't worried about that rule. Spot never left the ranch unless Gramp or he took him.

"Don't try to do too much," Gramp called as Bert left the house.

Spot had kept two anxious eyes upon his master. He stood up and watched questioningly as Bert went toward the gate.

"Come on," Bert ordered. "You're to help ride fence."

Spot didn't wait for Bert to open the gate. He made a short run, sailed over, and went dashing around the barnyard. He circled Bert until they came near the barn. Then he stopped running and walked quietly behind him. Outside the barn door he stopped while the boy went in to get his horse. He was still waiting when Bert led Blaze out. He watched expectantly, but he didn't leave his post until Bert called.

The boy rode across the pasture to the fence that divided it from the hayfield. He opened the gate, led his horse through, closed it again and remounted. He rode across the hayfield to the gate that opened into the south pasture and let himself through again. Then he rode southwest to the farthest corner of the pasture.

From there where his task began, Bert went east along the line fence. Whenever he found a wire that had come loose from a post, he dismounted and stapled it. He soon found that there were so many places where one or more wires were loose that it was easier to walk and lead his horse than to be forever mounting and dismounting. By the time the sun was straight overhead, he had gone little more than half the distance to the gate which marked the end of the section of fencing he had to repair. Mr. Henderson's men were responsible for the section that went from the gate east to the other end of the line fence.

Bert sat down and ate the lunch he had brought with him. He tossed half a sandwich to Spot. The dog caught it with

4

his usual expertness and swallowed it in one gulp. He waited expectantly for more.

"Go catch yourself a rabbit if you're still hungry," Bert told him.

Spot wagged his tail but made no move to leave. Bert grinned at him. He knew the dog would eat anything tossed to him, even though he wasn't really hungry.

Bert rested only a few minutes after he had eaten. He wanted to finish the job early so that he could get home and help Gramp unload the salt. He continued to find many places where the wires were loose.

"It's a wonder all of Henderson's cattle weren't in this pasture," he told Spot.

Bert was so interested in his work that he didn't hear the hoofbeats of the approaching horses until Spot's low growl warned him someone was near. He looked up to see Mr. Henderson and his foreman, Bill Stewart, riding toward the gate. Although the man was clean-shaven and wore his hair close-cropped under the big Stetson, Mr. Henderson always reminded Bert of pictures of Buffalo Bill. He had the same commanding appearance as he sat his horse. Bert could imagine the rancher riding into a herd of buffalo as confidently as he rode into a herd of cattle.

Bill Stewart presented a picture in sharp contrast to the ranch owner. It wasn't merely that Bill was a much younger man. It was the way he slouched in his saddle and seemed to take no interest in what went on around him. But whenever he looked at a person, he gave the impression of watchfulness. To Bert it seemed that Bill was suspicious of everyone he met.

"It's high time you were taking care of that fence," Mr. Henderson greeted Bert, and added, "There's a wire loose at that next post."

"When I get that one stapled, our part of the fence will be done," Bert answered trying to keep the resentment out of his voice.

"Have you seen any Bar 3 calves in your pasture?" Mr. Henderson demanded in a tone that seemed to say it was Bert's fault if Bar 3 cattle strayed.

"No." This time Bert didn't quite keep the anger out of his voice.

"We'll take a look," Mr. Henderson told him.

Any other rancher would have asked permission, even though he knew the permission would be granted. Bert made no move to open the gate as he would have done for another neighbor.

"If any Bar 3 calves are in our pasture," he said, "they got there through your part of the fence. I've been along all of ours and there are no signs that cattle got through."

He didn't look up to see the astonishment on Mr. Henderson's face. Few men had the courage to remind this overbearing man that he often neglected to keep his own share of the fences in repair. Bert would have been surprised if he had seen the smile tugging at the corners of Mr. Henderson's mouth.

Bill jumped from his horse and opened the gate.

"If you don't have any cattle in this pasture, I'll leave the gate open," he told Bert.

Bert nodded.

Apparently Mr. Henderson hadn't noticed Spot until he

had ridden through the gate. He pulled his horse to a stop and nodded at the dog.

"You keep that dog off my ranch or I'll shoot him," he threatened.

Bert choked back an angry reply. The two men rode off and he went back to his work.

It took Bert only a few minutes to finish. He tied his hammer to the saddle and swung himself onto the horse's back. He turned Blaze toward home, but reined in the horse after he had gone only a few steps. The boy sat there in frowning indecision. Even though Mr. Henderson deserved to be treated rudely, Gramp wouldn't approve of Bert's coming home without trying to help find the lost calves. Next to leaving a gate open, failing to help a neighbor look for strays, was as unfriendly an act as a person could do. Bert turned Blaze and rode east along the dividing fence.

There were some narrow valleys surrounded by steep hills in this direction. If cattle had broken through the fence, they might be in one of those valleys. As he rode along, Bert noticed that there were many places where the wires had come loose.

"Mr. Henderson ought to have his men take better care of his section," he said to himself. "No wonder his cattle stray."

He continued along the fence keeping a sharp watch on both sides of it. There was a possibility that the Bar 3 riders hadn't searched their own pasture well. When he reached the second of the hills, Bert noticed that the wires were slack and sagging above him on the crest. He knew what that meant. The wires were broken on the opposite slope. Soon he came to the top of the hill and now he could see that all four wires were broken. It was odd that all four were broken between the same two posts! It seemed even more odd when he found they were also broken at the foot of the hill. Usually wires broke along a slope or at the summit.

Reaching this second place where the wires were broken, Bert swung out of the saddle to take a closer look. He picked up one of the wires and gave a gasp of surprise. The strands had been cut! It wasn't until then that he noticed the truck tracks. What had happened was now clear. Someone had clipped the wires. Then a truck had been backed through the opening until the rear was against the hill that formed the north wall of the little valley. The wall had been used as a chute. Cattle had been driven down the hillside and into the truck.

"Rustlers!" Bert exclaimed in dismay. "Rustlers took the calves!"

He remounted at once, and sent Blaze racing in the direction that Mr. Henderson and Bill had gone. He crossed the pasture without catching sight of them. When he reached the gate between the pasture and the hayfield and found it open, he knew they were searching around the haystacks. The next moment he saw Bill. When Bill saw Bert racing toward him, he turned to meet him.

"Rustlers got your calves," Bert called as soon as he was close enough for Bill to hear him.

Bill listened without saying a word as Bert told what he had found. The foreman hesitated even when he'd finished, as if he couldn't believe what the boy had told him. Then he stood in the stirrups and shouted for the rancher at the top of his lungs. He continued to shout until there was an answering hail from Mr. Henderson. Bill and Bert rode toward the sound of the voice. When they reached the rancher, Bill reported what Bert had found.

"Show us the place," Mr. Henderson directed.

Bert led the way back to the valley where the wires had been cut. All three dismounted for a closer look.

"It was rustlers all right," Mr. Henderson agreed. "Someone who knows this area is in the gang. No one would stumble onto this place to load, not in the dark."

"I suppose whoever took the cattle scouted around here in the daytime," Bill suggested.

"Could be," Mr. Henderson nodded. "But it's strange none of you saw him. Who was in this pasture yesterday?"

"Speck Wilson," Bill answered. "He didn't mention seeing anyone around."

Bert hadn't noticed that Spot didn't follow him when he rode to find Bill and Mr. Henderson. The first he was aware that the dog was gone was when he heard the sharp yelp Spot always gave when he was driving cattle. Bert looked up. A small herd of yearlings, he judged there were ten or twelve of them, were trotting from the east. Spot was a few paces behind them.

Mr. Henderson saw the calves at the same time. "There are twelve they didn't get," he said and added, "Don't let that dog run my cattle."

Bert paid no attention to the rancher. "This way," he called to Spot, waving toward the gap in the fence.

Spot moved to the right of the herd. He quickened his pace until he was even with the leader. Then he moved closer. The calf turned and trotted toward the gap in the fence. Spot slowed his pace until he was following the last calf in the herd. He stayed behind the herd until the last Bar 3 calf was back on Bar 3 land.

"That's far enough," Bert called.

Spot turned away from the herd and trotted back to his master's side.

"I'll be doggoned!" Bill exclaimed. "He handled that herd better than most riders could."

"He did all right," Mr. Henderson admitted grudgingly, "but I don't want him running my cattle."

The rancher turned his attention back to the cut wires. With Bill's help he tried to pull the cut ends together and fasten them, but there wasn't enough slack for that. Bert went to his horse and got the small roll of wire he had on the saddle horn.

"Here," he said, "you can splice it with this."

"Good," Bill answered taking the wire.

"You fix these wires as well as you can, Bill," Mr. Henderson ordered. "I'll ride to the house and notify the sheriff. Be careful you don't tramp out those tire tracks. The sheriff might learn something from them."

"I'll go home and tell Gramp," Bert said.

Mr. Henderson jumped onto his horse and raced off. Bert turned Blaze toward home. The horse started off at an easy lope with Spot running behind. As he was crossing the top of the hill, Bert glanced back. Bill was hurriedly dragging the loose wires to a point between the two posts.

10

"The way he jumps around he'll have all of those tracks trampled out," Bert said to himself.

He crossed the south pasture and the hay land next to it. When he came to the pasture called the home pasture, he rode east from the gate. He had to ride all the way to the southeast corner of the pasture before he found the cattle his grandfather had put there. He rode slowly toward the herd until he was close enough that he could make a count. He stood in the stirrups to do it, using the method of counting by two's as his grandfather had taught him.

"There are fifty-four cows and fifty-two calves," he said aloud when he finished. "That means ten cows and their calves are gone."

Suddenly he felt sick. Mr. Henderson might be angered at the loss of twenty or thirty yearlings, but it would be no great hardship for him. To Gramp, however, the loss of ten cows and their calves would be a severe blow. Bert was ashamed of the selfish thought, but it would come. It might mean he wouldn't get to go to high school this year.

Without any real hope that the dog would find the missing cattle, Bert ordered him to fetch the others. Spot turned and trotted north and disappeared over a low hill. Bert swung Blaze around and followed. He gave a whoop of relief when he reached the crest and could see the missing cattle grazing on the low ground below. Spot was getting behind the herd to bunch them.

"Let them go, Spot," Bert called.

Knowing he could trust his dog, he turned Blaze toward home without waiting. He was so relieved to know none of their cattle had been stolen that he could hardly keep from yelling at the top of his voice. He hadn't realized how much time he had spent with Mr. Henderson and Bill. It was getting late. Gramp would wonder what had happened to him. He loosened the reins and let Blaze lope. Soon he heard Spot behind him.

When he had nearly reached home Bert saw two horses tied at the hitching post outside the ranch yard. He recognized them as two of the Marshalls'.

"Jim and Nancy are here," he told Spot as he swung off his mount. The dog looked up at him as if to say, "I could have told you that."

Much as he wanted to talk to Jim Marshall, his one close friend, Bert did not neglect to take care of Blaze first. As he hurried toward the house, he saw Jim and Nancy carrying blocks of salt from the pickup into the shed.

"Big news," Jim shouted. "We're—"

"I have bigger news," Bert interrupted. "Rustlers took twenty or thirty of Mr. Henderson's yearlings."

"How do you know it was rustlers?" Nancy demanded.

Bert told of his adventure with Mr. Henderson and Bill.

"I'm going in and tell your grandfather," Nancy said to Bert. "Anyway, carrying salt is no job for a lady."

"Since when have you been a lady?" her brother called after her.

Nancy didn't bother to answer. Bert and Jim took up the job of carrying the salt into the shed. His friend asked so many questions that Bert didn't get a chance to ask about Jim's news. Before they had the truck unloaded, Gramp came out of the house. The story had to be told again.

"That was done by a well organized gang," Gramp said

12

soberly when Bert had finished his account. "More of us will lose cattle."

"Mr. Henderson called the sheriff," Bert reminded him. "Maybe the rustlers have been caught by now."

"Walt Cameron is a good sheriff," Gramp said, "but catching that gang will be a big job. It isn't the way it was in the old days, when rustlers had to drive their cattle to a hiding place. Now they load them into a truck and have them at the market in one night."

"It's getting late, Jim," Nancy called to her brother as she came from the house. "We'd better go home."

"There are only a few blocks left," he answered. "I'll help finish the job."

"What was your big news, Jim?" Bert asked.

"We're to start branding tomorrow," Nancy answered for him. "And you're to help."

"Yippee!" Bert exclaimed. "Branding is the one ranch job that's fun."

As soon as the rest of the salt was safely stored in the shed, Jim and Nancy left. Gramp and Bert went into the house to eat their evening meal.

"Do you think we ought to guard our herd tonight?" Bert asked.

"The rustlers won't come back this close to last night's raid," Gramp answered confidently. "I wonder if they took any of our cattle?"

"Not from the herd in the home pasture," Bert assured him. "That much I know. I counted them."

"Good." Gramp looked pleased and relieved. "I stopped and left salt for the herd in the north pasture. I didn't count the cattle, but I would have noticed if there had been more than one or two missing."

"I hope the sheriff catches those rustlers before they get any more cattle," Bert said.

"You'd better get to bed early tonight," Gramp warned him. "Branding may be fun, but it's hard work too."

They both had a good deal to think about and were silent for the most part as they finished their meal.

2

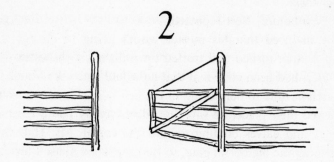

THE NEXT MORNING Bert was up before sunrise. Early as he was, Gramp was even earlier. Bert dressed and went to the kitchen. He started toward the door, but Gramp stopped him.

"I fed your horse," he said. "You'd better eat so you can get started."

When Bert came out of the house, Spot was waiting for him.

"You can go to the line fence with me," Bert told him, "but you have to come back and stay with Gramp. No dogs at branding."

Spot wagged his tail to say he understood. He went through the gate behind Bert and followed him to the barn. When Bert led Blaze out and mounted, Spot dashed around the barnyard, but as soon as Bert started, Spot followed quietly behind. When the boy dismounted to open the gate at the line fence, he turned to his dog.

"Go home."

Spot hesitated. He wagged his tail and gave a short plead-ing bark.

"Go home," Bert repeated.

Convinced that his master wasn't going to change his mind, Spot turned and trotted toward the ranch house.

Bert had been confident that he would reach the Marshall ranch in time to help bring in the first herd. However, as he neared their place, he saw the riders already had a herd of cows and calves coming toward the corral. Mr. Hall was opening the big corral gate, so Bert stationed himself nearby so that he could turn back any cows that tried to shy away. He turned to watch the riders driving the cattle.

Nancy was riding on the right side of the herd and Jim on the left. Mr. Marshall and Bill Stewart were behind the herd. Bert turned his head to see where the others were. Mr. Smith, whose own ranch was closer, was supposed to help and there ought to be two men from the Henderson crew. He saw Mr. Smith ride up to the corral on the other side, but there was no sign of any other man from Hender-son's than the foreman.

Bert turned his attention back to the herd. The cattle were moving ahead well. The first cow was almost to the open gate. Suddenly, with the perversity of her kind, she swerved and dashed away from it. Blaze seemed to guess the cow's intention. Before Bert could give a command, the horse leaped forward and blocked the cow's path. She was forced to turn back and go through the gate. The others followed meekly.

The moment the last cow was inside the corral, Mr. Hall swung the big gate shut. Mr. Smith climbed to the top of the corral. He walked along the wide board at the top until he reached the other end. Here he climbed down into the small corral. He went to the wooden gate between the two corrals.

His job would be to work the gate, so that as the others separated the cows from their calves, the cows could be driven into the small corral and the calves held in the other. Bert jumped from his horse and went to help.

When he reached Mr. Smith's side, the man handed him a long slender whip, then shoved the gate open wide enough to let a cow crowd through. As her calf tried to follow, Bert flicked the whip across its nose. The surprised creature backed off enough so that Mr. Smith could close the gate. As soon as another cow was in the right place, he let her through and again Bert drove the calf back. This was repeated with cow after cow. In spite of Bert's and Mr. Smith's efforts, occasionally a calf got through the gate. When that happened, Mr. Smith closed the gate and helped Bert give chase. Whichever of them caught the fleeing young one would hold it until the other came to his aid. Together they would throw the calf and drag it through the gate.

It seemed to Bert that it took a long, long time, but at last all the cows were in the small corral and the calves in the large one. Mr. Smith opened the outside gate of the small corral and Bert drove the cows out into the pasture. Mr. Smith closed the gate. Someone opened the gate between the two corrals and the calves were driven into the smaller one where it would be easier to catch them for the branding.

Jim brought the branding irons from the barn and put

them in the fire Mr. Marshall and Mr. Hall had started.
The others rested nearby while the irons were heating.

"Where's the other Bar 3 man, Bill?" Mr. Hall asked.
"I thought Mr. Henderson agreed to send us two of you."

"Mike and Tex are at the south camp," Bill explained.
"Speck was supposed to come with me, but he was in town
until late last night. He didn't feel up to coming."

"It really doesn't matter," Mr. Marshall assured him.
"We have a big enough crew. As long as you are here to
do the branding, I'm satisfied."

The others nodded approval. All of the ranchers liked
to have Bill do their branding. He seemed to know exactly
how to apply the hot iron so that it made a lasting brand
but never burned deep enough to cause a sore.

"How many Bar 3 cattle did those rustlers get, Bill?" Mr.
Hall asked.

"We're not sure," Bill answered. "We think they got
twenty-six head of yearlings."

"There had been reports of rustling in the counties west
of us," Mr. Marshall said. "I had hoped someone would
catch the rustlers before they moved into our neighborhood."

"Cameron will make short work of them." Mr. Hall
spoke with confidence. "He's a good sheriff."

"He's too fat to catch cold," Bill scoffed.

"Don't let his size fool you," Mr. Hall warned.

"Bring on the calves," Bill yelled. "The irons are hot."

Nancy, Jim, and Bert jumped up and dashed toward the
calves. There was always a race for the honor of bringing
the first calf to the branding fire. Last year Jim had been
first at every branding. This year Bert was determined it

would be different. He reached under the nearest calf and grabbed for the foreleg on the other side. The calf tried to squirm away, but the herd was packed so densely that there was no room for it to move. Bert got a grip on the foreleg with his right hand. He reached his left hand back and caught a hind leg. He pulled with all his strength and at the same time shoved against the calf's side with his shoulder. The calf was upset the way a football player is caught by a tackler. As the calf fell, it struggled to get free. Bert held on with all his strength, but the calf's free back hoof caught his wrist and broke his hold. Bert made a desperate grab and caught the leg again. He began to drag the calf toward the fire before it could struggle free. From the corner of his eye he saw that Jim was having even more trouble. This was one time Jim wouldn't win.

"The winner and champion cowboy," Bill shouted while Bert was still a few paces from the fire.

Bert looked up with a grin of triumph that quickly turned to a look of surprised disbelief. Nancy had already dragged her calf to the fire. Mr. Hall grabbed the calf's other two legs and helped the girl hold the struggling creature in position to be branded.

"She's the champion all right," he agreed loudly.

There was no smile of triumph on Nancy's face. She turned her face away as Bill pressed the red hot branding iron against the calf's shoulder. The calf gave a frightened bawl. Nancy seemed scarcely able to keep her hold as the smell of burning hair and scorched hide rose into the air.

"Let him go," Mr. Hall ordered.

Nancy loosened her hold and jumped back as the calf scrambled to its feet. It trotted away as if nothing had happened. But Nancy didn't start toward a second calf. She stumbled away from the fire with her hand over her mouth. Suddenly, she turned toward the ladder that led to the top of the corral. As she scrambled up, she called back that she was supposed to help her mother get dinner ready. Jim laughed so hard that he let his calf get away.

"Nancy's a good cowboy until she smells burning hair and scorched hide," Mr. Marshall chuckled. "Then she's just another girl."

For a time after Nancy left, the work went on rapidly. Bert, Jim, and Mr. Smith caught the calves and dragged them to the fire. As soon as ten were branded, they were separated from the others and driven into the pasture to find their mothers. A mark was made on the gate for each group turned out. At the end of the branding they would have a tally of the number of calves. As more and more calves were driven out of the corral, there was more room for the others to dodge the catchers. It became harder and harder to corner one.

The sun broiled down on the scene. The scampering calves stirred up a cloud of dust so thick it seemed to hold the smell of burning hide and hair so that the workers were never free but drew in that sickening odor with every breath. At last Mr. Smith got his rope. He cast a noose on the ground in front of a scampering calf. He gave the rope a flip. The noose seemed to jump from the ground and grab the calf's front legs. Mr. Smith gave a jerk on the rope and the calf fell to the ground.

Jim grinned and nodded at Bert. Together they hurried to the other side of the corral and got their ropes. They had spent several Sunday afternoons practicing and here was a chance to show how well they could use them. For some reason, with calves scampering around the corral, they weren't able to do nearly so well as they had when they practiced. Occasionally, one of them managed to catch a calf and trip it to the ground; far more often they failed. The whole crew had a good laugh when Jim caught a calf with a noose so large that the calf stepped through it and Jim jerked the noose tight around the calf's chest. The calf dragged Jim around the corral until Mr. Smith and Bert managed to catch hold of the rope. The combined weight of the three of them dragged the calf to a stop.

"This is too slow," Mr. Marshall called. "Smith, you and Hall rope the calves and let the boys drag them to the fire."

Now the work was speeded up, but even so it was almost noon by the time the last calf had been branded and turned into the pasture.

"Shall we bring in the other herd now?" Bill asked.

"We might as well," Mr. Marshall answered.

But at that moment Nancy appeared at the top of the corral. "Dinner's ready," she called.

"In that case we'll eat first," Mr. Marshall grinned. "We wouldn't want to make the cooks mad."

"I'd starve to death in another hour," Jim insisted.

Bert had always thought that the meals served at branding time were ample pay for the hard work that had to be done. Today's spread was no exception. The table was loaded with heaping platters of such food as was guaranteed to fill them up. Nancy and Mrs. Marshall moved around, watching to see that the plates of the men were constantly refilled. By the time he had eaten the big slice of apple pie the rancher's wife served for dessert, Bert felt he was too full to move.

All the time they were eating, the men talked about the rustlers. Bert was encouraged by the fact that most of Gramp's neighbors seemed to believe Sheriff Cameron would soon nab them. Bill was the only one who expressed any doubt about the sheriff's ability. He wondered if the Bar 3 foreman talked that way merely to keep the other men arguing. It certainly kept things lively.

"Let's get the other herd in so we can finish before dark," Bill suggested, pushing back his chair and rising to his feet.

"Give us a few minutes to rest," Jim protested. "I'm too full to move."

"Stay there and rest," Nancy said quickly. "I'll take your place on the drive and you can take mine as dish washer."

"We'll all take a short rest," Mr. Marshall said. "Branding will go faster this afternoon."

Both Nancy and Jim rode with the drivers when they went to bring in the herd. The drivers were Mr. Marshall, Bill, and Bert. They all went off, leaving Mr. Hall and Mr. Smith to bring that morning's herd to a different pasture.

"I'll race you to the top of the hill, Bert," Jim challenged.

"I don't think we ought to run our horses now," Bert objected. "They may have to do a lot of chasing when we start the herd."

"You're afraid I'll beat that old plug of yours," Jim scoffed.

"You say, go, and I'll show you whose horse is a plug," Bert retorted.

"Hold on, you two," Mr. Marshall cautioned. "There'll

be no racing now. The horses will have enough running to do while we're bringing the herd in."

The horses went on at an easy trot until they had circled to the other side of the herd. For a few minutes then there was considerable dashing about as the cattle were bunched and started toward the corral. As soon as they were moving well, the riders took the places Mr. Marshall had assigned. Bill rode on the left side of the herd near the front, with Bert a dozen paces behind. Jim had the position opposite Bill, and Nancy the one opposite Bert. Mr. Marshall rode drag.

The cattle moved ahead so willingly that none of the riders had much to do. All of them were taken by surprise when the cow in the lead made a sudden lunge to the left and tried to lead the herd in a dash to escape.

Like the others, Bill had been giving little attention to the herd. He didn't see the cow make her attempt to break away until his horse wheeled and lunged to cut her off. The horse's sudden turn almost threw Bill from the saddle. He struggled to regain his balance, but there was no time. The horse's feet slipped and he fell heavily on his side.

Bert had seen Bill's horse start to turn. Horse and rider had cut off his view of the cow, but he didn't need to see her to know what was happening. Such a thing had occurred too many times before. He urged Blaze to a gallop, ready to hold the other cattle while Bill rounded up the one that was trying to escape. He gave a cry of alarm when he saw Bill's horse fall. Had the foreman kicked free?

Bert had never seen a rider dragged, but he knew that was a real danger when a horse fell. He leaned far over Blaze's neck and shouted, "Get him."

Blaze responded to the urgency in his master's voice. He leaped forward as if he had been thrown from a catapult. There was a wild scramble up ahead as Bill's horse struggled to get up and get going. Bert couldn't see whether Bill had kicked his feet free of the stirrups but it didn't look that way. There was no time to hesitate. If Bill's foot was caught, the horse had to be brought under control before he could start to run.

Blaze was almost even with Bill's horse when the excited animal got his footing. "Hold him," Bert ordered.

Blaze was in mid-air in a tremendous leap when Bert gave his order. The horse stiffened his front legs and came down with a jolt that snapped the boy's head back and almost tore him from the saddle. Desperately he grabbed leather with one hand and braced himself in the stirrups. He leaned over and with his free hand grasped the reins of Bill's horse. As he straightened up, Bert snubbed the reins around his saddle horn, holding the other horse's head so close that he could hardly move.

"Easy, boy," Bert called softly.

Mr. Marshall and Jim had seen the danger at the same moment that he had. They, too, had done their best to race toward Bill. As Bert pulled Bill's horse to a stop, Mr. Marshall and Jim leaped from theirs. They ran to the other side of the horse where it was now clear Bill was caught and pulled the foot free of the stirrup.

"Are you all right?" Mr. Marshall asked anxiously.

Bill put his right foot on the ground and tested his weight on it. "It hurts, but I'm sure the bone isn't broken. If it was, it would be no more than I deserve for going to sleep on the job."

"How lucky Bert reached you so quickly!" Mr. Marshall said.

Bill limped around the horse and came to the boy's side. "You saved my life," he said holding out his hand. "I couldn't pull my foot free. It had me sweating, I can tell you. I'd have been dragged if you hadn't caught my horse."

While the embarrassed Bert was trying to answer, Jim came to his rescue.

"I'm glad we didn't race." He grinned. "The way that old Blaze took off he would outrun any horse."

"He's a good horse." His master patted Blaze's neck affectionately.

"Let's help Nancy get the cattle to the corral so we can finish branding," Mr. Marshall said.

As soon as she had seen that Bill was safe, Nancy had started rounding up the cattle that were starting to stray. She had turned the runaway cow back and now had the herd moving again. Bert noticed that Bill checked his saddle girth and hesitated before he swung himself back into the saddle.

It didn't take long to get the herd into the corral. Bert wasn't surprised to see the cow that had caused the trouble lead the others through the gate. There was always one that took over.

It was almost sundown by the time the last calf was branded.

"Do you want us at the Bar 3 tomorrow, Bill?" Mr. Marshall asked as he gathered up the branding irons.

"Yeah," Bill replied. "Mike and Tex are bringing the herd from the south pasture today."

"From there we'll go to your place." Mr. Marshall turned to Bert.

"We'll be ready," Bert assured him. "I'll be glad when all the calves are branded. That ought to stop the rustlers."

"The Bar 3 calves they took were yearlings and had been branded last year," Mr. Smith reminded him.

Since they went in the same direction, Bert and Bill left together. They let their horses jog along at an easy pace. Bert tried to start a conversation, but the foreman seemed to be occupied with his own thoughts. The silence stretched out so long that the boy was glad to reach the fork where they would part.

"I'll see you in the morning," Bill called as Bert turned toward home.

"I'll be there," Bert answered and waved. He loosened the reins to let Blaze lope.

Bert had hardly started down his fork when his dog rushed down the road to meet him. Spot circled the horse once and then trotted contentedly behind.

When he came within sight of the ranch yard, Bert saw a car parked at the yard gate. He felt a chill of fear; he recognized it as Sheriff Cameron's. The fact that the sheriff was here must mean that rustlers had taken some of their cattle.

In spite of his anxiety, Bert took care of his horse, and romped with his dog who'd had a lonely day, before he went into the house.

26

3

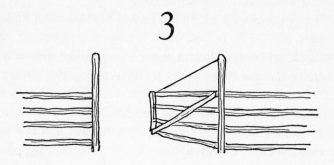

His grandfather and Mr. Cameron were on the porch, talking, but Bert couldn't make out what they were saying. There was a break in the conversation when he stepped onto the porch.

"Hello, Mr. Cameron."

"Hi, Bert," the sheriff said. "How did the branding go?"

"We finished at the Marshalls and will go to the Bar 3 tomorrow."

Supper was soon ready and Gramp and Mr. Cameron sat down at the table where three places had been set. They waited for Bert to wash up, then Gramp got up and went to the stove to dish out the food. Bert wanted to help him.

"You sit down and rest," Gramp ordered. "You've done enough for one day."

"I'm too hungry to wait until you get the food on the table," Bert protested with a grin.

"Didn't the Marshalls feed you at noon?" the sheriff asked.

"They could feed him at noon and twice in the afternoon and he'd still be hungry now." Gramp laughed.

Bert joined in the laugh, but he was glad that Gramp had fixed a big meal. It had been a long time since he had helped empty those platters at noon and he had done a lot. Even the thought that rustlers had taken some of their cattle didn't keep him from being hungry.

"How many of our cattle did they get?" the boy demanded when he saw that neither Gramp nor the sheriff was going to volunteer the information.

Gramp gave him a puzzled look.

"Oh," he said after a pause. "You think the sheriff is here to investigate rustling. He is, but it isn't about our herd. We didn't lose any cattle."

Bert cast an inquiring look at Mr. Cameron. He was surprised to see the sheriff shifting about uncomfortably.

"Well, you see, Bert," the sheriff said lamely, "I thought your grandfather might know something that would give us a clue to the rustlers."

"Go on and tell him, Walt," Gramp snorted angrily. "If he has to learn that I am suspected of being in with the rustlers, he'd better learn it from you."

Bert shoved back his chair and jumped to his feet.

"Who says Gramp is a rustler?"

"Take it easy, Bert," Sheriff Cameron answered quietly. "No one has accused your grandfather. There are a couple of circumstances that look queer. I want your grandfather to explain them so there won't be any silly talk."

Bert looked from the sheriff to Gramp. Slowly he sat down.

"What things need explaining?" He tried to speak as quietly as the sheriff had.

Again Sheriff Cameron shifted uneasily in his chair. He cast an appealing look at Gramp, but Gramp was looking at his plate and pretended not to notice.

"Well," the sheriff explained, "some of the missing calves were found in your pasture."

"I'm the one who found them," Bert said, "or rather Spot did."

"I know." The sheriff nodded. "But someone is sure to say they represent your grandfather's part of the theft."

"You wouldn't care if they did," Bert pointed out shrewdly. "That would be just silly talk. There must be something else."

"I'd rather the boy heard it from you, Pete," the sheriff said, looking at Gramp.

"You're telling it." Gramp was acting stubborn.

"Yesterday, when your Gramp was in town, he paid off a five-hundred-dollar note at the bank. I know he hasn't sold any cattle."

This time it was Gramp who pushed back his chair and got angrily to his feet. He strode across the room to the telephone on the wall.

"What are you doing?" the sheriff demanded.

"I'm going to call Mr. Campbell at his house and explain a few things to him," Gramp snapped. "He knows dealings between a banker and his customer are confidential."

"Don't be so all fired hasty, Pete," Sheriff Cameron cautioned. "I didn't learn that from Mr. Campbell. You know that in this state all notes for more than three hundred dollars have to be recorded with the county clerk. There was a record of yours being released."

Gramp turned away from the telephone and came back to the table.

"I've lived on this ranch a good many years," he said. "You know I'm no thief."

"Of course I know you're no thief," the sheriff agreed. "But as sheriff I have to investigate all possible clues. I have to investigate my friends as well as other people."

"I know, Walt," Gramp agreed, calming down. "Let's forget it and enjoy our meal."

Bert waited for Gramp to explain how he had paid off the note at the bank. Now that he was no longer angry, he wouldn't hesitate to do so. But Gramp didn't explain, nor did he try to start a conversation about anything else. To break the long drawn out silence, Bert told about Bill's accident. He carefully stressed the fact that it was Blaze's quick action and prompt obedience that saved Bill from serious injury.

"Blaze is one of the best horses in this community," the sheriff said, "but even a good horse has to have a good rider to do a thing like that."

"Bill ought to spend more time getting the sleep he needs, and less time hanging around town at nights," Gramp snorted. "I'm surprised Henderson keeps him as foreman."

"He's a good man otherwise," Sheriff Cameron pointed out mildly. "Henderson has to overlook some faults."

The two men now seemed to have forgotten their earlier differences. They chatted about ranch affairs in the way they usually did when they were together. Yet, in spite of their apparent friendliness, Bert felt something was wrong. Gramp seldom lost his temper, but he had certainly lost it a few minutes ago. It wasn't likely that he would forget his anger this quickly.

The sheriff arose to leave and Bert walked to the car with him. Spot met them at the door, but Bert ordered him to stay in the yard.

"A dog can cause a lot of trouble in cattle country," the sheriff said as he opened the car door and slid behind the the wheel.

"Spot won't." Bert was sure of his dog. "You notice he stayed in the yard when I told him to."

"What will he do when you're not here to give the orders?"

"Spot won't get into trouble," Bert insisted.

Sheriff Cameron seemed about to say something more, but changed his mind. He reached forward to turn on the ignition.

"You know Gramp wouldn't have anything to do with rustlers," Bert said.

Sheriff Cameron agreed. "If he wasn't so confounded stubborn, he'd tell me where he got the money to pay off the loan. Then I could stop any silly talk I heard. Rumors can do a lot of harm when a community is stirred up about something as bad as rustling."

Bert nodded but didn't say anything. The sheriff gave him a keen look. An understanding smile spread across his face.

"I know better than to ask you," he said. "Even if you knew, you wouldn't tell me, and I wouldn't want you to."

He turned the key and started the motor. Bert watched

the car swing around. The big man could do things fast when he wanted to.

"Keep that dog out of trouble," the sheriff called as he drove out of the yard.

Bert continued to stand and watch the car until the gleam of the headlights disappeared behind the hill. Then he went slowly toward the house. A feeling of uneasiness was nagging at him. Why would anyone suspect Gramp of being in with the rustlers? It was natural that Gramp wouldn't tell the sheriff how he happened to have the money to pay off the note at the bank. It really wasn't any of the sheriff's business. "But why didn't Gramp tell me?" Bert asked himself. "He always discusses ranch business with me." He was immediately ashamed of the thought. Whatever Gramp's reason, it was a good one.

Bert was so tired that he went to bed at once. He half awakened when Gramp went into the room on the other side of the hall, but immediately he fell back into a deep sleep. Later, some sound awoke him fully. He listened intently. Someone was moving about in the kitchen. Bert's first thought was to call Gramp, but he brushed that aside. If he called out, he would frighten the intruder away. Carefully he slid out of bed. His bare feet made no sound as he stepped into the hallway.

In the dim light Bert could see into Gramp's room. Gramp wasn't in bed. Bert heard the kitchen door close quietly and he heard Gramp speak to Spot. Bert was glad that no one could see the look on his face. There must be something wrong with his head, or he would have realized at once that no prowler could sneak into the house with

32

Spot on guard. He opened his mouth to call to Gramp to wait for him, but he didn't call. Evidently the sheriff's visit had upset Gramp so much that he couldn't sleep. Bert returned to his room and crawled back into bed.

When Bert awoke again, the room was light. For some reason he felt relieved to hear Gramp working in the kitchen.

"I fed your horse," Gramp said cheerfully when Bert came into the kitchen.

Gramp seemed to have forgotten the sheriff's visit. He whistled for all he was worth as he cooked their breakfast and put it on the table.

"I'm going to set those posts in the south fence today," he announced as Bert was preparing to leave.

"Why don't you wait until next week? We'll be done branding and I can help you. Setting posts is a lot easier when two work together."

"There'll be other things to do next week. There always are on a ranch."

Bert knew it would be useless to argue. He opened the door and stepped out into the yard where Spot was waiting for him.

"You can come part way," Bert told him. "Then you'll have to come back and keep a watch on things."

Spot understood. He wagged his tail, took a few excited jumps, and sailed over the gate. He dashed around the yard as Bert walked toward the barn. When Bert went inside, Spot crouched beside the door.

On the ride across the pasture and through the hayfield, Spot dashed around as excitedly as a small boy on a picnic.

When they reached the gate that opened into the Henderson place, Bert ordered the dog to go home. Spot looked up at him with such a pained expression that Bert had to laugh.

"The next thing I know," Bert told him, "you'll be crying when I tell you to do something that you don't want to do. Now go home."

Spot gave his master another accusing look, but when he saw that Bert wasn't going to relent, he turned and trotted toward the ranch.

Mr. Smith was at the Henderson corral when Bert arrived. He and Bert helped the Henderson hands start separating the cows from the calves. In a few minutes Mr. Marshall and Jim joined them. By the time the calves had been separated from their mothers, Bill had a fire blazing brightly. Mr. Henderson brought the branding irons from the tool shed.

"One of the irons is missing," he said.

"It won't matter," Bill answered indifferently. "Four will be enough."

"I'm going to get the first calf today," Bert challenged, as he and Jim waited for the irons to heat.

When Bill called for calves, Bert dived for the one nearest. He missed the calf's foreleg and it edged away from him. By the time he grabbed the next one, Jim had already thrown his calf and was dragging it to the branders. Strangely, none of the men noticed who was first. There was no praise for Jim's accomplishment nor teasing for Bert because he had been beaten.

As the work went on, Bert became more and more aware

34

that missing was the bantering and joking that usually went on when a gang of men worked together. Instead, the men went about the job as if it were some grim task that had to be endured. During a brief rest, while some of the calves were let out of the corral, Bert had a chance to talk with Jim.

"What's the matter with everybody today?" he demanded.

"I guess they're thinking about the rustlers, The raid on Borden's yearlings last night is proof that the rustlers aren't afraid of Sheriff Cameron."

"At Borden's!" Bert exclaimed. "I hadn't heard that. Gee, that's close to us."

"No closer than Henderson's," Jim reminded him. "Borden's joins you on the east and Henderson's place on the south."

"We have cattle in the pasture next to Borden's," Bert said. "That makes it seem closer."

Jim and Bert were called back to work and didn't get a chance to talk together again until the crew stopped at noon. At the table all the conversation was about this last raid by the rustlers. Bill seemed the only one who didn't believe someone in the community was a member of the gang. Bert was shocked to hear Mr. Smith suggest that Sheriff Cameron was either protecting the gang or afraid to tackle it.

"Omaha or Denver is the nearest market," the man said. "From here it's more than a twelve hours' drive for a truck to either place. The sheriff ought to be able to catch them in that time or at least get word to the authorities at the markets to be on the watch."

"I've known Cameron for a long time," Mr. Henderson said. "He's not afraid to do his job and he certainly isn't protecting any rustlers."

"That's right," Mr. Marshall agreed. "This gang is well organized, but they'll make a mistake and Walt will get them."

"I hope he gets them before any more of us lose cattle," Mr. Smith grumbled.

When the men returned to the branding, the sun did its best to make the work disagreeable. It beat down on the branding corral, heating it like an oven. The dust kicked up by the scurrying calves hung chokingly close to the ground. This job, usually one of exciting fun, today was miserable drudgery for Bert and for the others. Once Jim challenged him to a race to see who could catch the next calf, but there was no real fun in the contest. Bert hardly realized that for once he had beaten Jim.

While he held the calf Bill was branding, Bert noticed the spot on the ground where a hot branding iron had been dropped. The marks —3 were still plain in the dust. Bill lifted the hot iron from the calf and dropped it to the ground. He and Bert jumped up and the calf scrambled to its feet and dashed off. Bert watched idly as Bill bent down and picked up the hot iron to put it back into the fire. By some odd chance the iron had dropped at almost the same spot as the mark left by the first one. However, it had fallen so the mark was reversed from the other. The second 3 had almost closed on the 3 left by the earlier brand. If it had fallen a quarter of an inch closer, it would have made a new brand, —8—. "That would be a good brand," Bert said to himself as he turned to catch another calf. "The Bar 8 Bar."

By the time he had dragged the calf to the fire, all marks in the dirt had been trampled out. Bert forgot about the odd brand made by the iron as the work dragged along.

Finally, the last calf in the herd had been branded. It was almost sundown.

"We should finish my other herd tomorrow," Mr. Henderson said. "Bert, be sure to tell your grandfather we'll be at your place the next day."

"We'll be ready," Bert answered as he had before. With the others he went toward their horses.

When he returned to the Henderson ranch the next morning, Bert told Mr. Henderson that Gramp would be ready for the crew the following day. "We'll need only one man from your crew."

"That's fine," Mr. Henderson said. "My men are late with some of the work. I'll be glad to have them on the job at home."

Things went much more smoothly than they had the previous day. No one had heard of any rustling the night before. Bert wondered if this wasn't the reason the work seemed less tedious than it had. Of course, the fact that the rustlers hadn't made another raid didn't mean that they had moved to a different area. The men were relieved enough to do some clowning. They joshed the boys.

Late in the afternoon there was a brief stop while the branded calves were driven out of the corral. Bert had dragged the last calf to the fire. There were enough men at the gate and he wasn't needed, so he dropped down to rest.

Bill got up and went over to his jacket hanging on a corral post. He was in such a hurry to get his tobacco out of the jacket pocket that he forgot the iron he had just used. It was lying on the ground where he had dropped it. Bert picked the brand up to put it back into the fire. As he reached out toward the glowing coals, he remembered the mark he had seen the day before. "I wonder if it really would work?" he said to himself. "I guess I'll see what I get." Placing himself so he had a firm thrust, he pressed the iron into the dust. When he lifted it, there was a plain —3 mark. Carefully he turned the iron around. He leaned over so he could see what he was doing as he put the iron down beside the first mark. This time when he lifted the iron, he saw it had made a new brand. The two 3's were so close together that they formed an 8, with a bar on either side.

"Bar 8 Bar," he said aloud. "That would make a good brand."

He took a quick look around to see if anyone was watching. No one was. He rubbed the brand out and put the branding iron back into the fire.

Bert waited impatiently for Bill to come back to the fire so that he could show him how the brand could be changed. However, Bill was having trouble rolling his cigarette. By the time he had it made and lit, it was time for Bert to catch another calf. After he had caught a few calves, Bert came to the decision that he should tell Mr. Henderson how easily the Bar 3 brand could be altered. But when he did get a chance to speak to the rancher, Bert changed his mind. He was afraid Mr. Henderson would laugh at him.

He started home after the branding was done without having told anyone of his idea.

On the way home, Bert thought of the brands again. He had heard ranchers tell about rustlers changing brands in the old days. But would changing brands work now? Today there were brand inspectors to check branded cattle. If there was a question about a brand, an inspector would be called to check it before the cattle were sold. Bert decided he would tell Gramp his idea. At least Gramp would know if it was possible for rustlers to change brands and get away with it.

Again Bert was startled to see the sheriff's car parked in the yard when he got home. This must mean some new trouble. He reached out to open the door of the porch, relieved to hear Gramp and the sheriff talking quietly. His relief vanished when he heard Gramp's words.

"I didn't want the boy to have the dog, Walt," Gramp was saying, "but a boy out here on a ranch needs some companionship besides that of his grandfather. That dog has not been running cattle. He doesn't leave the ranch unless Bert takes him."

"You never can be sure of dogs, Pete," the sheriff answered doubtfully. "I had a report of a dog that looked like Spot running cattle on the Markham place."

Bert suddenly realized he was eavesdropping. He yanked the porch door open and let it slam behind him.

"Spot hasn't been chasing any cattle," he said angrily.

"Wait a minute, Bert," Gramp cautioned. "You haven't greeted our guest yet."

"Hello, Mr. Cameron," Bert said more quietly. "I didn't

39

mean to be rude, but I got mad when I heard Spot accused of doing something I know he didn't do. I trained him, and I'll be responsible for him."

"Your grandfather has assured me that Spot wasn't away from the ranch last night. I suppose it was some other dog that chased Markham's cattle."

"I'm glad I'm not the sheriff," Gramp chuckled. "It seems to me troubles keep piling up for you—rustlers and dogs chasing cattle."

Sheriff Cameron smiled and shrugged his shoulders as he got to his feet.

"There have been times when I wished I had more to do," he said. "This isn't one of them. Well, I'll be getting along."

"Aren't you going to stay and eat with us?" Gramp demanded. "Wasn't that last meal good enough?"

"Too good." The sheriff laughed, rubbing his ample stomach. "I have to watch my weight."

After he and his grandfather had finished their meal, Bert got a sheet of paper and a pencil.

"I think I know how the rustlers hide the cattle they steal," he said. "They change the brands."

He laid the paper on the table and drew the —3 brand on the sheet of paper.

"If the brand is reversed and applied carefully," Bert explained drawing the new brand to make his explanation clearer, "there would be a new brand—like this."

The boy sketched the reversed 3 and the bar so they made an 8 with one bar before it and another after it. "Now we have a Bar 8 Bar," he said.

"I never heard of such a brand." Gramp was indifferent. Suddenly his manner changed. "It might work," he exclaimed. "A good brander could do it. The second brand could be a reversed 3. Fitted against the other 3 it would make a brand that read Bar 8. I've heard of that brand."

"Don't you think that must be the answer?" Bert asked. "The rustlers rebrand the yearlings, wait for the new brand to heal, and then take them to market."

"No," Gramp pointed out. "It sounds possible, but it wouldn't really work. As you know, we have brand inspectors today. Besides, where would the rustlers hide the calves while the new brands were healing?"

"There must be some place where they can hide them," Bert insisted.

Gramp merely shook his head. "Maybe, boy, maybe."

If Gramp didn't know of a possible hiding place, there probably wasn't any. Still, Bert made up his mind that the next time he saw Sheriff Cameron, he would share his idea. The sheriff might know things he and his grandfather didn't; perhaps even a hiding place Gramp was not aware of.

4

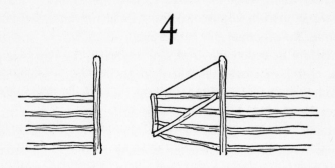

THE NEXT MORNING Bert was up even before Gramp.

"What are you doing up so early?" Gramp wanted to know when he heard Bert tiptoeing out of his room.

"I'm going to have the cattle in the corral when the others get here," Bert said.

"It'll be easier if you wait until some of them come along to give you a hand," Gramp pointed out.

"I'll have Spot help," Bert replied. "Besides, he needs more training."

"All right," Gramp agreed. "Breakfast will be ready when you get back."

Bert held the yard gate open for Spot to go through. The dog raced after him and jumped about so excitedly he must have understood this was a special day. As usual, he stopped romping and walked quietly at Bert's heels when they approached the barn.

Bert put feed in the boxes for the two horses. He saddled

Blaze and got the bridle on him before he had finished eating his grain. When he started to lead him from the barn, Blaze snorted in disgust because he had not quite finished eating. Bert soothed and patted him.

Before he rode away from the barnyard, the boy swung the corral gate open so that it would be ready when he brought the herd in. The moment he saw some of the cattle, Bert knew something was wrong. Instead of most of the animals being close together with only a few stragglers, as there should be this early in the morning, they were scattered about in small groups. Spot following close, Bert rode to the first group of cows and calves. He couldn't see that anything was wrong. He rode from group to group and still didn't find anything.

"Bunch them, Spot," he ordered.

Spot trotted to the cattle farthest away. He circled them and then moved up behind so that they started ahead. Bert turned to a small bunch and brought it toward the others. In a short time, with Spot's help, Bert had all the cows and calves strung out in a long herd walking toward the corral. He drew up his horse and raised himself in the saddle. Quickly he counted. There were sixty-five cows and sixty-three calves. That was what there should be. Next, Bert turned his attention to the yearlings. Almost the moment he began counting, he knew some were missing. When he finished, he found there were only twenty-five yearlings. There should have been twenty more.

With a sinking heart Bert turned Blaze toward the east boundary line. "Get the others," he called to Spot.

Obediently the dog left the herd and trotted toward the

east fence. Before he had gone more than a few yards, Bert turned Blaze to the northeast. There was only one place in this pasture where cattle could be loaded into a truck. It would save time to look there first. From the top of the hill that formed one side of a small ravine, Bert could see the place where the fence crossed the ravine. As he had feared, the wires were cut. Before he reached the bottom of the incline he could see the tracks left by heavy tires. A moment later he saw where the yearlings had been driven down one side of the ravine and loaded into a truck backed up to the bank.

Bert wanted to dismount and examine the tracks, but he knew that would be a waste of time. The rustlers might be caught if he went back to the ranch at once and Gramp called the sheriff. He wheeled Blaze about and sent the horse racing back the way they had come. Spot heard the galloping and raced to meet them.

"Bring the herd in," Bert called to the dog.

Bert slowed Blaze to a trot as he neared the herd. As soon as Spot had trotted close to the last cow Bert turned his horse to circle around the herd so that he wouldn't turn the cattle from their course. Again he urged the horse to a gallop.

Gramp had heard the pounding hoofbeats and came hurrying from the house by the time Bert reached the yard gate.

"What's wrong?" he asked anxiously.

"Rustlers got twenty of our yearlings." Quickly Bert told what he had found.

"Come in and eat your breakfast. I'll call the sheriff."

Bert was still eating when Gramp came back to the kitchen.

"He's going to try to catch the truck, but I don't suppose he'll have any better luck than he has had in the past."

"It's too bad he doesn't do more patrolling at night," Bert complained.

"He was patrolling last night. He was so confident the rustlers would raid in a different direction he was patrolling the Hester ranch."

Bert finished his breakfast in a hurry. He would have liked to stay in the house and wait for a call from the sheriff, but he needed to get back to the herd. He knew Spot would do his best, but one dog couldn't be expected to bring in a herd alone. If the cows were kept from scattering, he would be doing well.

As Bert came out of the yard, he saw Mr. Smith tying his horse in the corral. At the same time a yell came from the northwest. Bert turned and saw Jim and his father riding into the ranch yard.

"Who's bringing in the cattle?" Mr. Smith called from the corral.

Bert looked toward the east. The herd was coming toward the corral as steadily as if three or four riders were driving it.

"Spot is," he answered. "I'll help him. The rest of you tend the gate."

Swinging himself onto his horse, Bert wore a pleased smile. He was lucky to have such a dog. He found him trotting alertly behind the cattle. Whenever one tried to turn back, Spot dashed in front of the troublemaker and forced her to return to the herd.

45

"Good work, Spot. Keep them coming."

Bert hurried alongside until he reached a position near the head of the herd. Here he would be ready to turn back any cattle that tried to shy away from the gate. Only one made an attempt to escape, but Bert turned her back without any trouble. In a few minutes the entire herd was in the corral and Mr. Smith had closed them in.

"I wouldn't have believed that a dog could handle a herd of cattle that well," he said in admiration.

"I'm glad you didn't bring him to the Bar 3 with you." Speck Matthews laughed. "If Mr. Henderson found out that a dog can handle cattle as well as riders can, he'd fire us."

Bert was surprised to see Speck on hand to help with the branding. This would be the first time Mr. Henderson had sent two men, and he'd specially said they needed only one.

Bert started the fire and placed the branding irons near it. He thought to himself how easy it would be to change the B over Bar to a Box B merely by putting new lines around the brand. He drew a B on the ground and added the three lines to make a ⬚B⬚ . He decided he would point out to Bill how the rustlers could change the —3 and B brands. Maybe Henderson's foreman could convince the men that this was how the rustlers were hiding their cattle. When he looked around to tell him, he realized he hadn't seen the Bar 3 foreman with the other men.

"Where's Bill?" he asked.

"He went into town last night," Speck answered. "When he came back, he must have gone to the south camp to check the herd there. Anyway, he didn't come back to the bunkhouse. It was getting time to start, so Mr. Henderson had me come over to take his place."

"Your grandfather will have to handle the branding irons, then," Mr. Marshall told Bert. "He and Bill are the only ones who can brand the way it ought to be done."

Gramp had stayed in the house to help Nancy start the noon meal. Mrs. Marshall would come over later to take charge, but there were things Nancy could get done ahead of time. Bert went to the house to get him.

"Did the sheriff call again?" he asked as he and his grandfather returned to the corral together.

"No," Gramp shook his head regretfully, "but of course it is really too early to expect a call from him."

The others were separating the cows and the calves when Bert and his grandfather got back to the corral. Gramp went to tend the fire while Bert helped the others. When they had a moment together, Bert told Jim about the yearlings that had been stolen during the night. The word was quickly passed around among the men so that by the time the cows had been driven out of the corral, all the men knew of the loss. They gathered around Gramp to express their sympathy and anger.

"If the sheriff doesn't get results soon, we'll have to organize posses of our own," Mr. Marshall said.

"What's Bill doing today, Speck?" Gramp asked trying to turn the conversation to a less unpleasant subject.

"He didn't come back from town last night," Speck explained again. "I suppose he rode over to the south camp to look at the herd and didn't get back to the main ranch in time to come over here."

"My guess is, he was in town playing poker," Mr. Smith suggested. "I've heard he's been seen with some of the professional gamblers."

"He plays poker sometimes," Speck admitted. "He's come home several times with a pocketful of money that he says he won in poker games."

"I'm surprised that Mr. Henderson keeps him." Mr. Marshall was disapproving. "I wouldn't want a foreman who spends so much time in town at night that he isn't ready to do his work the next morning."

"Bill's a good man," Gramp said. "He can do a job when he sets his mind to it. You all know that. I suppose Henderson keeps him in the hope that he will outgrow his foolishness."

"I wouldn't want a man who hangs around professional gamblers," Mr. Marshall insisted. "He's too apt to end up in serious trouble."

"The irons are hot," Gramp announced, changing the subject.

Speck, Jim, and Bert started toward the calves. Today there was no race to see who would catch the first one. Everyone was too occupied with thoughts of the rustlers. The men realized that the loss of twenty yearlings was a severe blow for Mr. Weston. They realized, too, that their ranches might be the next to be raided.

Bert could hardly wait for the morning's work to be done. Several times he had turned toward Gramp to ask permission to ride out to the north herd to see if cattle had been taken, but he was needed in the corral. They were done with that first herd in time for them to bring in the other herd before noon, otherwise he didn't know how he would have borne it.

"I'm anxious to see if the rustlers took yearlings from that herd, too," Bert told his grandfather.

"There's no place to load them in that pasture," Gramp reminded him.

Bert took out after them like a released spring all the same. Although he knew Gramp was right about the ease of loading, he was greatly relieved when he and the others reached the herd and he had counted the yearlings. All of them were there.

"I'd like to see Spot handle this herd," Jim suggested.

"I think he can." Bert called to his dog, "Bring them in, Spot." Spot trotted off obediently. An especially independent cow, with a calf beside her, was the objective because she had wandered the farthest. She watched him until the dog was directly behind her. Suddenly, she wheeled and charged him, head down. Spot dodged out of the way.

"He can't even handle one cow." Jim chuckled.

"Watch," Bert told him.

Spot had run only two or three steps. Now he whirled and started toward the cow. The cow slid to a stop. As the dog continued toward her, she turned and trotted in among the others, making sure that her calf was at her side. Spot left her and gathered in other stragglers, gently, without frightening them. In a surprisingly short time, the cattle were bunched and started toward the ranch yard.

"Spot's better than any rider I ever saw," Jim admitted generously. His admiration was sincere. "It would have taken two riders longer than that to round up the herd."

As the lowing beasts approached the corral, Bert saw that no one had opened the gate.

"Circle them and open it up, Jim," Bert called. "Speck and I will help Spot put the herd in."

They were ready for that desperate moment when their charges want to swerve away, and the two easily cut off their escape. Somehow the independent cow managed to be at the end, but she passed and Jim swung the gate shut. Bert and Speck dismounted and climbed into the corral to help separate the cows from the calves. They had almost finished when Gramp, Mr. Smith, and Mr. Marshall came to help them.

"We had a meeting," Gramp told those at the corral.

"The sheriff has been having so much trouble catching the rustlers that we want to find a way to help him," Mr. Smith added.

"Did you think of a plan?" Jim asked.

"Not a very good one," his father answered. "We are going to suggest to the Protective Association that everyone ride herd at night."

"That'll be all right for a while," Bert pointed out, "but it won't take long before everyone will be tired out and a lot of the ranch work won't get done."

"We know that," Gramp agreed, "but we have to try something."

Branding was finished early in the afternoon. While the men were standing about the corral chatting before leaving, Jim suggested that Bert have Spot do some tricks.

"He doesn't do fancy ones," Bert objected.

"That one with the hats is pretty clever," Jim insisted. He turned to the grinning men. "Give me your hats."

Jim took the ones they reached out to him. He carried them to the other side of the corral and set them in a row on the ground.

"Get Bert's hat," he ordered.

Spot dashed to where the hats were set, all looking so similar. It seemed as if he picked up the first hat he came to, but when he returned and dropped it at Bert's feet, it turned out to be Bert's own hat.

"Pretty clever," Speck said, "but I'll bet he wouldn't bring mine if you told him to."

"He wouldn't, because he doesn't know you," Bert agreed. "But he knows Jim and Nancy. We'll have them hide. You tell me which one you want him to find and he'll find the one you choose."

"Now you're kidding me," Speck said.

"I'll show you." Bert laughed. "I'll take Spot into the barn while they hide. When I bring him back, you tell me which one to send him for."

Bert took Spot into the barn. When Speck called that Nancy and Jim were hidden, Bert and the dog returned to the corral.

"Have him find Nancy," Speck said.

"Find Nancy!" Bert ordered.

Spot bounded off at once. He went around the corral and out of sight. Bert and Speck climbed to the top of the fence so they could watch. Spot raced straight to a clump of shrubs. He gave an excited bark as Nancy stepped out of her hiding place.

"All right, Jim," Speck called and Bert's friend crawled out from under the small pile of hay where he had been hiding.

"He went right by Jim and straight to Nancy." Speck

couldn't get over the feat. "He understood what you said all right."

Mr. Smith and Speck mounted their horses and left soon after. Mr. Marshall and Gramp continued to talk over plans for catching the rustlers. Nancy and Jim chatted with Bert while they waited for their father. Bert told them of his idea about how the rustlers must be changing the brands and then hiding the calves nearby.

"That must be just what they are doing," Nancy agreed excitedly. "You ought to tell the men."

"I did tell Gramp," Bert said. "He doesn't think the rustlers could do that, because someone would notice that parts of the brands had been put on later."

"If they had a good place to hide the yearlings for a couple of weeks, the brands would heal enough so that a person would have to look real close to see parts of them had been made at a different time," Jim said. "I think you've hit on the way they are working."

"I expect Sheriff Cameron will come out later today," Bert said. "I'll talk to him about it."

After the Marshalls left, Bert and Gramp loaded the things they would need into the pickup and drove out to repair the cut fence. Before they had finished the job, Sheriff Cameron drove up.

"When you weren't at the house and the pickup was gone, I figured you'd be out here repairing the breaks," he explained.

Bert studied the sheriff. It was amazing how much the man knew about the ranches around here. He really knew the layout of the county where he was officer. He had driven directly to where they were working, without having to follow the roundabout way they had taken with the truck. That took real figuring. For the first time Bert was persuaded his theory about the rustlers and how they worked might be foolish. If there was a hiding place where they could hold the cattle long enough for the new brands to heal, surely Sheriff Cameron would know about it. Still it would do no harm to put his idea before the officer.

The sheriff talked to Gramp a few minutes, examined the tracks left by the truck, and started back toward his car. Bert took a couple of steps in his direction. "Maybe the rustlers rebrand the cattle they steal," he blurted out.

The sheriff turned and came back to Bert and Gramp.

"I had thought of that," he said, "but the cattle they steal are yearlings. They were branded nine months or a year ago. The changed brands could be spotted easily."

"I know," Bert agreed, "but if they had a place to hide the cattle for a couple of weeks, the brands would heal enough so that a person would have to look closely to see they had been changed. Look how easy it would be to change our brand."

He got a small stick and drew the B on the ground. Then he drew three more lines and changed the Ḇ to a B̄ . He drew the —3 and showed how it could be changed to a —8— by reversing the —3. "From B over Bar to Box B, and from Bar 3 to Bar 8 Bar without any trouble at all," he said.

But the sheriff wasn't entirely convinced. "It would be easy to see that the brands had been changed," he insisted.

"I know," Bert agreed, "but I still think those brands

would heal quickly, and before long only an expert could tell that they had been changed."

"That still leaves the matter of a hiding place," the sheriff pointed out. "The only possible place would be the Carter ranch. It has some rough ground that isn't pastured this year, but the Bordens are making hay on the hay land. They'd notice any unusual activity."

Bert thought to himself that even the Bordens might be suspected. He knew their ranch owned three or four brands. They might own the very ones that these could be changed to. The fact that they had claimed they lost cattle to the rustlers wasn't proof of their innocence. It would be a simple thing to rebrand some of their own cattle and put them with the stolen ones. While he was turning these thoughts over and trying to decide whether or not to mention the possibility to the sheriff, Gramp seemed to read his mind.

"Don't suggest that the Bordens are the rustlers," he said. "They're honest people. Besides, they've made even more money than Mr. Henderson. They have no reason to steal."

"Whoever the rustlers are, we'll catch them," Sheriff Cameron vowed as he went to his car.

After the officer left, Gramp and Bert finished repairing the cut fence. They picked up their tools, put them in the truck, and started back to the ranch house. On the way Bert ran over in his mind all the out-of-the-way rough land in the community. The only likely place for a hide-out was indeed that land on the Carter ranch, and the sheriff had pointed out that it was almost impossible for the rustlers to be using it.

5

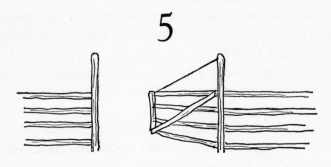

Next day the crew took care of the calves at the Smith ranch. It was the last of the year's branding. Ordinarily, Bert looked forward to these times of being with the others and was sorry when the job was through. But now he was glad to be done with it; he knew the others were too. They all had too much to worry them. The ranchers were intent only on how quickly they could finish and go back to guarding their own threatened stock. The usual fun was missing.

Before he started home, Bert called Jim aside.

"Let's take a look at the Carter place tomorrow," he suggested. "We can take fishing tackle and our lunch. After we've searched for the rustlers' hiding place, we can try for some bass in the lake."

Jim grinned at him. "Trust you to combine fishing with any trip."

"We might not find the rustlers and we wouldn't want to waste the day," Bert said with an answering grin.

"There's one drawback." Jim hesitated. "If I go, Dad will insist that Nancy goes too."

"That's no drawback," Bert answered. "She's as good a fisherman as either one of us. Besides, we'll get her to cook the fish. How's that?"

"She might be in the way if we spot the rustlers."

"No, she won't. If we do, we'll hurry in with the news. She can ride as fast as we."

"Since you don't object to Nancy's tagging along, I'm all for it," Jim agreed. "I'll get Dad's permission right now."

"Gramp has been wanting me to take a day off," Bert told him. "He'll let me go."

Jim talked to his father briefly and returned to report that he and Nancy could go.

Bert was up just as early next morning as he had been on the others. The truth was he liked to be stirring then, when everything was so fresh. Gramp was preparing breakfast when he looked in. He was pleased that Bert was to have a day's outing with Nancy and Jim. He even hunted up his two favorite bass plugs for him to take.

"You'd better dig some worms and take along hooks," Gramp advised, as Bert was making for the barn to feed his horse. "If the bass aren't hitting, you may be able to catch some pan fish."

Bert was fastening the last of his equipment to his saddle when Nancy and Jim rode into the yard.

"I prefer bass," Gramp called to them as they were leaving, "but if you can't catch bass, I'll settle for pan fish."

"We'll bring you some kind of fish," Nancy promised.

The three rode east to the Borden fence. Instead of taking

the road northeast to the Borden house, they rode straight east across that pasture. They crossed three more pastures before they reached the Carter ranch. They entered it through a gate that led to a hayfield dotted with stacks of hay.

"It's been quite a while since they finished the cutting." Jim looked around the hayfield. "The rustlers could have been hiding here a couple of weeks without anyone seeing them."

"That's about as long as they have been raiding in our neighborhood." Bert gave a low whistle.

"As far as that goes," Jim's narrowed eyes showed he was thinking deeply, "they could have been here before the haying, moved out temporarily maybe."

"Let's fish before we look for signs of rustlers," Nancy suggested uneasily. "We'll be too scared to do any fishing if we find they're around."

"We have to cross the rough land to get to water," Bert reminded her. "If their hide-out is here, we'll know it before we reach the lake."

"Wouldn't it be great if we caught the rustlers!" Jim exclaimed, brandishing his fishing rod as if it were a gun.

As soon as they had crossed the meadow, they separated so they could search the narrow canyons of the rough land. If the rustlers were holding stolen cattle here, one of them would surely see some.

As they separated, Bert had his first feeling of misgiving about having Nancy with them. What if she were the one to find the rustlers' hiding place? He shrugged the thought away. If she did find it, she would do just what he or Jim would do, turn back and get the others.

Bert was riding slowly down a narrow, deep ravine when he heard Nancy call to him. He answered her, but he had to ride ahead until he found a place where Blaze could climb up the bank. Nancy was waiting for him at the top of the hill.

"Jim found something," she told him.

She turned her horse and started down the steep hill. Bert followed after, wondering. When they reached the foot of the hill, they had to search for a slope their mounts could manage. Bert found one not too steep for the horses. He went ahead calling to Nancy to follow him. At the top of the hill they could see Jim in the valley just beyond. He had ridden his horse about half-way down the hill and left it there while he walked the rest of the way to study the signs on the ground. They'd better do the same. Bert and Nancy left their horses beside Jim's and scrambled down the hill to join him.

"They've been loading and unloading cattle here," Jim said, pointing to the markings.

Bert saw the well-worn trail that had been made by a truck backing up to this natural holding place. There were marks that must have been made by a loading chute. Nails had been driven into the trees surrounding a grassed area. Though now pulled out, they had left neat holes. It was plain someone had built a corral by nailing poles to the trees.

"That corral hasn't been gone long," Bert observed, looking closely at the marks on the trees.

"I'd say it was still being used when the Borden crew started haying in that meadow," his friend replied.

"I wonder why the rustlers tore down the corral and left?" Nancy asked.

"They must have been afraid someone in the Borden haying crew might come this way and find it," Bert answered.

"The big question is, where did they move to?" Jim said.

"Maybe we can follow the truck tracks and find their new hide-out," Bert suggested.

"We might," Jim agreed. He glanced toward the horses as though he were trying to decide whether it would be better to ride along the trail, or walk. He turned abruptly to Nancy. His tone was curt and anxious. "You didn't ground rein your horse."

"It won't matter," Nancy said. "Princess won't leave the others."

"She might if she got scared." Jim frowned. "Anyway, you know you are supposed to tie or ground rein a horse when you leave it."

"I know," Nancy was contrite. "It won't happen again."

"Let's get the horses," Bert suggested. "We may have to follow the tracks a long way. Anyhow, if we find the rustlers' hide-out, we'll be in a hurry to get away from here."

Nancy and Jim nodded in agreement. The three turned and started up the hill. They had climbed only a few steps when they were startled by the sudden sharp crack of a gun and the angry whine of a bullet over their heads. They dropped to the ground as if someone had jerked their feet from under them. As he fell, Bert saw the bullet plow up the dust at the horses' feet. The frightened animals pulled

59

back. Finding that there was nothing to stop her, Princess dashed up the hill and disappeared. Blaze and Jim's horse tried to follow her, but their trailing reins prevented them from running.

"We'd better catch our horses before they get away," Bert whispered urgently.

He and Jim turned their heads and looked back. They could see no sign of the person who had fired the shot. Still they hesitated. That shot had been close. It took all of Bert's courage to force himself to his feet. Even then he crouched to make himself as poor a target as possible. He didn't need to look back to know that Nancy and Jim were following him.

"Steady, Blaze," Bert called as he neared his horse.

Jim's horse tried to sidle away, but the boy made a desperate lunge and caught the reins. He swung himself into the saddle. Then he kicked one foot out of the stirrup and reached a hand down to Nancy. She put her foot in the stirrup, grabbed Jim's hand and swung herself up behind. Bert had moved over to help Nancy onto Jim's horse. When he saw she didn't need his help, he mounted and led the way across the top of the hill and far enough down the other side that they would be in no danger of being hit by a second shot fired from the same place.

"Do you suppose we ought to circle around behind that hill to see if we can find out who fired that shot?" Bert sounded doubtful.

"We'd better get away from here," Jim answered. "The shot was meant to scare us and our horses. The next one might do more than scare us."

"That's right," Bert agreed soberly.

They rode along the hillside until they were quite sure they were a safe distance from whoever had fired at them. Then they rode to the top of the hill, where the horses could travel more easily. They had ridden a mile or more along the crest of the ridge before Jim reined in. Purposefully he turned.

"We ought to find Princess so the rustlers won't get her," he said.

"If I had only ground reined her as I should have!" Nancy lamented.

"What's done is done," her brother answered.

"I think we'll find her at the last gate we came through," Bert said. "Runaway horses usually head for home."

They urged their mounts ahead at an easy lope. Jim and Nancy often rode double, so Jim's horse was accustomed to the extra burden. Nancy gave a cry of relief when they came within sight of the gate and saw Princess standing there.

"Maybe we ought to circle to the west and go to the lake," Jim suggested.

"Oh, no," Nancy protested. "Whoever shot at us might find us there."

"That's right," Jim agreed before Bert could speak. "Besides we ought to go home as quickly as possible, so Sheriff Cameron can be notified of what we found."

"Let's ride to our house," Nancy suggested. "It isn't any farther to circle north of the Borden place to our place than it is to go south of it to Bert's home."

"Suits me," Bert agreed. Maybe Nancy was nervous. If she were he did not blame her.

As soon as they were through the gate, they again put their horses to an easy lope. As he rode along, Bert turned over in his mind the meaning of the shot. There was the possibility that someone had been hunting out of season and the shot coming near them had been accidental. But he knew this was unlikely. Anyone hunting illegally would have been keeping a sharp watch for a game warden. He surely would have heard them talking and he would have seen them. They had made no attempt to stay quiet or hide, not realizing how right Bert's surmises had been. The shot had been meant to scare them, or even hit one of them.

When they rode into the Marshall ranch yard, Mr. Marshall hurried from the barn to meet them. He knew they would not have returned from a fishing trip this early without some good reason.

"We found the rustlers' hide-out," Nancy called to him.

Jim and Bert gave the rancher the important facts in brief.

"I'll call the sheriff," he said immediately and hurried into the house. The boys cared for their horses as they watched him go, wondering what would happen. They appreciated the need for haste. If only once the sheriff could get to a rustler location in time!

Mrs. Marshall gave them her usual warm smile when they followed her into the house. "You haven't eaten your lunches yet, have you?" she asked. "It would have been too early."

"We were so excited we forgot all about them," Nancy told her.

"Bring them to the kitchen table," her mother suggested. "Maybe I can find something to add. You've all had a full morning and must be very hungry."

"I'll fetch everything," Bert volunteered.

He hurried out to the horses and took the lunches from the saddlebags. Mr. Marshall had finished his talk with the sheriff and was in the kitchen when Bert came in again.

"Sheriff Cameron is taking some men and going out to the Carter land," he told them. "He thinks you youngsters have found the rustlers' hiding place all right."

The young people then filled in all the details of the morning's adventure while Mr. and Mrs. Marshall listened intently or plied them with questions.

As soon as he had finished his lunch, Bert got up to leave. He was eager to tell Gramp about their discovery.

"Maybe we can go to the lake tomorrow," he called as he mounted his horse. "The rustlers will be gone."

Gramp listened without interrupting as Bert told of the experiences he and Jim and Nancy had had. But Gramp wasn't as hopeful as Bert had been that the sheriff would catch the rustlers.

"Your guess about their hiding the cattle near where they stole them was right," Gramp admitted. "But they've moved to a new hiding place in a different locality."

"Then why shoot at us?" Bert demanded.

"I would guess the rustlers had left something there that might tell who they are," Gramp answered. "The shot was to scare you off before you found it."

"Then the sheriff and his men ought to find it," Bert pointed out.

Gramp shook his head. "Whatever it was, they've probably moved it now."

"I suppose the sheriff won't get our cattle back." Bert sighed.

"I haven't given up hope," Gramp said.

Bert and his grandfather spent the rest of the afternoon repairing fences near the ranch yard. As they worked, they talked about the need to watch the cattle that night. They decided that even if the sheriff didn't catch the rustlers, he would alarm them enough so that they wouldn't make any raids in the vicinity.

Before they quit that evening, they had the last of the fences repaired. With them in good condition, everything was caught up. There would be a few days in which there was little to do. Bert decided he would suggest a trip to the lake. The rustlers wouldn't make a raid during the day. He and Gramp would be back in plenty of time to ride herd at night.

When they returned to the house, Gramp went inside to prepare their supper and Bert went to the barn to take care of the horses. As Bert was having a romp with Spot after finishing his chores, the sheriff drove into the yard. Bert felt like shouting when he saw the car was full of men. The sheriff had caught the rustlers! But when he came closer, he saw that all the men were armed and none was hand-cuffed. These were the men the sheriff had taken along to help him.

"We didn't catch the rustlers," the sheriff said. "They'd been there, but they had moved on."

"Then Bert had figured out the way they operate," Gramp said.

The sheriff nodded.

"Why did they shoot at us?" Bert demanded.

"We saw signs that they had loaded a horse into a trailer," Sheriff Cameron answered. "We figured it was a horse that you youngsters might have recognized. The rustlers didn't want you to see it, so they scared you off."

"If we had had a little more courage, we would have found the rustlers!" Bert exclaimed, and added, "Maybe it was my fault we didn't. Jim wanted to circle around for another look, but Nancy seemed nervous and insisted that it was too dangerous and so I didn't back him up."

"You were right," Sheriff Cameron told him. "Men who rustle cattle are dangerous. You notice we're all armed."

When the sheriff and his men had left, Gramp went into the house to call the Marshalls and warn them that the sheriff hadn't caught the rustlers. While Gramp was talking, Bert took the food from the stove and put it on the table.

"You were right about the way the rustlers were operating," Gramp said. "If I had listened to you, we might have caught them."

"They had moved most of their things by the time I thought of that idea," Bert reminded him. "Anyway, the sheriff didn't think I was right either."

"Now the problem is to find their new hiding place," Gramp said. "Sheriff Cameron doesn't think there's another hiding place in this county. I'm afraid he's right."

Bert didn't answer. Gramp and the sheriff certainly knew this big county better than he did. They had been in every part of it. The sheriff, especially, seemed to know every valley, hill, and canyon. If the rustlers' hiding place was in another county, it would be even more difficult to find.

Gramp had Bert tell of their morning adventure again.

"I guess we can't learn much from what happened," Bert said when he finished.

"The sheriff learned some things." Gramp thought for a moment. "And perhaps he overlooked a few. But let's forget about rustlers. I've been thinking that we might get the Marshalls to go with us for an overnight trout fishing trip to Winding Creek."

"Gee, that would be great!" Bert exclaimed. "You know how I love to fish. Still, I didn't know how you'd feel under the circumstances. How can we leave our ranches now?"

"There isn't any work to be done," Gramp shrugged. "You know we are caught up. I can get Mr. Smith's brother-in-law, Harold Jenkins, to look after the ranch while we are gone. Mr. Marshall can surely find someone."

"Would Harold ride herd at night?"

"He would if it was necessary. But it won't be. The sheriff and I are convinced the rustlers will hold off on any more raids in this neighborhood for a few days."

"Then I'm ready," Bert declared. "How soon can we go?"

"It will take a day to get things lined up," Gramp answered. "We'll plan to start the day after tomorrow."

It wasn't until he was about to drop off to sleep that night that Bert thought about where Winding Creek was. Gramp had described it to him once before when they had planned a fishing trip that they hadn't been able to take. Gramp had told him that it was in a valley so narrow it was almost a canyon. There were other streams in other valleys in the neighborhood, but Gramp had told him Winding Creek had the best trout. Now Bert wondered if Gramp hadn't planned this trip with the thought that the rustlers might have their new hiding place in one of those narrow valleys. Probably he hadn't. If he had, of course he wouldn't have suggested that Mrs. Marshall and Nancy go along.

Next morning Bert and Gramp took the pickup to the Smith place. His wife told them that Mr. Smith and Harold were fixing fence, so they had to drive into the pasture to find them. Mr. Smith readily agreed to let Harold go. This was their last day of fencing. Harold was glad to have another job, even for a few days.

From the Smith ranch they drove to the Marshalls'. Bert wondered if Gramp hadn't planned the trip so that they would arrive there about noon. He knew Gramp was almost as fond of Mrs. Marshall's apple pies as he was.

When Gramp suggested the fishing trip, Nancy and Jim were eager to start at once. Even Mr. and Mrs. Marshall seemed enthusiastic. Mr. Marshall immediately went into the house to telephone to neighboring ranches to find someone to stay at his ranch while they were gone. By the time Mrs. Marshall asked them to come to the table, he had called every possible person and had been unable to get anyone.

"I guess that means we can't go," he said.

"You and the youngsters go," Mrs. Marshall urged.

"You'll be gone only a couple of days. I can look after the ranch that long."

"I wouldn't leave you here alone now, even if I do think the rustlers won't make any raids for a few days," Mr. Marshall answered.

"You go, Dad," Nancy urged. "I'll stay with Mom."

"No." Mr. Marshall shook his head decisively. "You and Jim may go. Mom and I'll tend the ranch."

Gramp was plainly disappointed. He suggested every possible person in the neighborhood, but Mr. Marshall had already called most of them. Of those he didn't call, none was able, he knew, to look after his ranch. Bert thought Gramp would call the trip off entirely. To his relief, though, Gramp said they'd take the trip anyway.

"We'll pick you up early tomorrow morning," he told Nancy and Jim. "Have everything ready."

"Don't worry about them." Mrs. Marshall laughed. "They'll probably be waiting for you before you leave home."

6

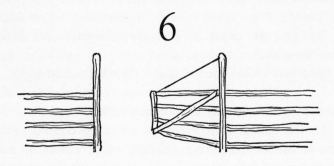

Eʀʟʏ ɴᴇxᴛ morning Gramp and Bert loaded their camping equipment, food, and fishing gear into the pickup. Bert had been afraid they would have to wait for Harold Jenkins, but he came to the ranch before they had everything ready.

"We'll leave Spot with you," Bert said. "If you have any trouble with the cattle, he'll be a big help."

"I know he's a smart dog," Harold answered, "but I wouldn't know how to handle him. You'd better take him with you."

Bert was surprised when Gramp agreed Spot should go. "He deserves a vacation. Let him come along."

Jim and Nancy were waiting when Gramp and Bert drove up. It took only a few minutes to put in their gear. Bert got some straws ready, so they could draw to see who would ride in the cab with Gramp, but Gramp waved for Nancy to get in beside him.

"Spot can ride up here too," he said. "You boys get in

back with the freight." Spot was so plainly pleased, he hoisted himself sedately up the steps. They had to laugh at him.

Bert and Jim settled themselves comfortably on bedrolls with their backs against a folded tent. They found they had a good view of the countryside as the truck rolled along.

For a while the land on either side of the route was very similar to that around their homes. There were the same wide, flat valleys surrounded by low hills. Gradually the appearance of the territory changed. The valleys became narrower and the hills steeper until they were going through country where the hills were so steep that Gramp had to shift gears to keep the truck from stalling. At home there were only the trees the ranchers had planted for windbreaks. Here there were many trees beside the streams that ran across the narrow valleys. Gramp stopped the truck at one such water course. He climbed down from the cab and the others joined him.

"There are good trout in this stream," he told them, "but more people fish here. Winding Creek is harder to reach so we are more likely to have it to ourselves. However, you three decide. We'll fish at whichever place you choose."

"Let's try Winding Creek," Jim urged. Bert and Nancy nodded in agreement. "That's where we started for; we have not been there and—well, there are plenty of reasons."

"Let's go," Gramp said and climbed back into the cab.

"Gramp, you're a faker," Bert said to himself as he and the others returned to their places on the truck. "You knew we would choose Winding Creek."

After he had settled himself, Bert took to wondering why

he had felt so sure Gramp wanted to go to Winding Creek.
He knew his grandfather so well, that he often understood
what was going on in his mind. "He knows it's the best fishing," he said to himself and dismissed the matter from his
mind.

It took longer to reach Winding Creek than Bert had expected. Gramp had told him how far it was from the ranch to
the place where they would camp. He felt as if they must have
gone that far and more before they stopped at the first
stream. They continued for what seemed many more miles.
This road had a surprising number of vehicle tracks con-
sidering the few ranch houses along it.

"It looks as if everyone goes to Winding Creek to fish,"
Jim commented uneasily.

"It's been about three weeks since we had any rain,"
Bert reminded him. "When it is dry for so long, a couple
of cars or trucks going over the road makes it look as
though there had been a parade. We have not actually seen
much traffic."

"Well, I don't want to have to push anyone out of the
way so I can fish," Jim grumbled.

Bert leaned over to look down the road they were following. Just ahead of them was a fork. One fork slanted to the
northwest; the other went almost straight north. Gramp took
the less-traveled one that went north. Here he had to drive
with extreme care. The road was little more than a trail.
It clung to the sides of steep hills. The grades they took were
unnerving. There were places where the truck tipped dangerously. It seemed that the least extra jar would send them
rolling to the bottom of the hill. At last Gramp brought the

truck to a stop under some trees. They pleasantly shaded a stretch of a small stream.

"This is Winding Creek," he announced as he climbed from the cab. He flexed his arms. "That last stretch was rough."

Bert and Jim grabbed their fishing gear and hopped down. Neck and neck, they raced to the creek. But when they glanced back and saw Gramp and Nancy starting to unload the camp gear, they looked sheepishly at each other. Without a word they returned to the truck and helped with the unloading. As soon as that job was finished, Gramp started a small cook fire.

"I'll fix the first meal," Nancy offered.

"Fine," Gramp agreed. "The boys and I will put up the tents."

Nancy's small one was quickly set up. Putting up the large one that Gramp and the two boys would use proved more difficult. But by the time it was up, the sides securely staked, and the important things stowed Nancy had the meal ready. While they ate, they discussed plans for the day's fishing.

"This afternoon we'll catch just enough for our evening meal," Gramp said. "After supper, we'll catch some for breakfast."

"I hope the fishing is good!" Jim exclaimed.

"It will be," Gramp promised. "Tomorrow we'll catch enough fish so that we can take some home with us."

They decided that this first afternoon they'd try downstream as Gramp remembered that stretch as having the best fish. To be fair they would draw straws to determine which section each would have for his own.

"I want to stay near camp this afternoon," Gramp told them. "If there are no objections, I'll fish the first section."

"That'll suit us," Jim said.

Nancy drew the shortest straw which meant she would fish the second section. Bert pulled the longest straw which left Jim the section between him and Nancy.

"I'll take my dog with me," Bert said. "He'll be company on the walk back to camp."

"Let's have Spot stay with Nancy," Gramp suggested. "There may be snakes. He'll watch for them."

Bert agreed readily. It was true that Spot would be company on the walk back to camp, but he might be a nuisance while fishing. The dog adored chasing rabbits. It would be like him to chase one across the creek just when the trout were hitting.

Bert and Jim walked with Nancy to where she would start fishing. As they went along, they caught grasshoppers and put them in small jars they carried for that purpose. Before he and Jim started on down the stream, Bert offered to put one of the grasshoppers on the hook for her, but Nancy laughed at him.

"What do you think I'm going to do?" she demanded. "Hunt up one of you boys when I want my hook baited?"

When Bert ordered Spot to stay with Nancy, the dog was contented to follow her.

"Wasn't that a little strange—your grandfather wanting Spot to stay with Nancy?" Jim asked as he and Bert walked toward their sections. "I wonder what he really has in mind."

"Girls are more afraid of snakes than boys are," Bert answered. "I would have offered to leave Spot with Nancy, but I was afraid he might be a nuisance while she is fishing."

"Nancy can handle snakes as well as any boy." Jim said.

Bert hadn't thought of that, but now that his friend had mentioned it, he knew it was the truth. He had seen Nancy kill a rattler as expertly as a boy would do it. In this area, where rattlesnakes were fairly common, anyone who spent any time out of doors had to know how to avoid them and how to kill them when it became necessary. So Gramp hadn't really been thinking of the danger of snakes when he suggested that Spot be left with Nancy. He had had some other danger in mind.

"I'll bet Gramp expects to find the rustlers' hiding place somewhere near here!" Bert exclaimed.

"That's what I think," Jim agreed. "I don't believe he places their hideout along Winding Creek or he wouldn't have brought us here, but maybe he thinks it is in some canyon nearby."

"This canyon would make a good hide-out." Bert glanced across the narrow valley with its tree-lined stream and steep hills. "Instead of fishing I'll scout downstream."

"I'll go with you," Jim told him. "Your grandfather and Nancy will catch enough fish for supper. We'll do our fishing tomorrow."

It was easier to carry their fishing rods than leave them and have to follow the stream back to pick them up. They might have good reason not to return the same way. They might be in a hurry. They hadn't given any thought to the noise they were making up to then. There was no need for quiet until they came to where they would fish. Now they moved carefully. In some places there were only a few trees along the stream; in others the trees grew thick. Anywhere under the leafy layer there were thick growths of shrubs. They could have traveled faster by going around and walking in the grass, but they chose to stay among the trees. If the rustlers were using this canyon as a hide-out, they might have someone watching at the top of one of the hills. By staying under cover the boys were doing the wisest thing even if it delayed them.

Bert judged that they had gone two miles before they saw any cattle. They both caught sight of the yearling herd at the same time. Bert glanced triumphantly at Jim.

"It seems we've found them," he whispered. "Let's take a closer look."

Jim nodded and they went forward again using extreme caution. They crouched low and moved from the shelter of one clump of shrubs to the next. They were almost on the herd before they realized there was a fence between them and the yearlings. They crept up to the barrier. From there they could see the brands on the cattle.

"They're all branded K," Bert whispered.

"That's the Kesterson brand," Jim said. "This fence must be the western boundary of their ranch. I did not realize anyone'd be likely to keep stock around here."

"Then these aren't stolen cattle." Bert was keenly disappointed. "When we spotted the herd of yearlings, I was sure we had found the rustlers' new hide-out."

"Me too," Jim agreed. "But it's certain there won't be a hide-out on the Kesterson place. We might as well go back and catch some trout."

"Yeah," Bert answered. "Tomorrow we'll fish upstream. We may find something there."

They turned back and walked a short distance together. When he saw a likely looking pool, Bert turned toward it while Jim continued farther along.

Bert selected a large grasshopper from his jar and put it on his hook. It made an excellent trout fly. He lifted the rod and moved the limber, jointed pole back until it was behind his shoulder. He snapped his wrist so that the tip of the rod whipped forward. The line played out from his reel sending the grasshopper sailing toward the creek. It lit on the pool almost as lightly as it would have if it had been leaping for a blade of grass and overshot the mark. At the moment the grasshopper fell to the water, there was a tremendous splash as a trout leaped to grab the offering. Bert felt a violent tug on the line. He hadn't been quite ready for this sudden strike. He let the line slip through his fingers as he grabbed for the handle of the reel. He reeled in swiftly, but there was no second tug on the line. When the hook came in sight, it was bare. The trout had taken the grasshopper, and the slack line had let him shake loose from the hook.

"I'll get you this time," Bert vowed as he put another grasshopper on the hook.

He cast a second time almost to the same spot he had aimed at before. This time he was ready. He was pulling gently on the line when the grasshopper fell to the water. Again there was a tremendous splash and a sudden tug on the line. Bert gave the line a slight jerk to set the hook. There came a terrific pull as the hooked trout dived for deep water. Grudgingly Bert paid out line. He felt the line slacken as the trout turned and raced to leap into the air. Bert reeled desperately. But when the trout fell back to the water and dived, the boy had to pay out most of the line he had taken in.

The trout repeated the maneuver. When he dived again, he acted as strong as he had when he had first been hooked. It seemed to Bert that these alternating dives and leaps continued for a long time, but at last they became shorter until finally he was able to keep the fish from diving. He worked the trout near the shore and lifted him out onto the bank.

"Boy!" he exclaimed aloud. "He's a two-pounder if I ever saw one."

Bert took the trout from the hook and stowed it in the canvas creel he wore hanging from his shoulder. He put another grasshopper on the hook, but he didn't drop it in this same pool. He knew the commotion he had made landing the fish would scare the others into hiding. It would be a couple of hours before they would feed again. He would have to find another pool for his next attempt.

He moved upstream until he found another likely looking place. He made a careful cast, but he misjudged the distance to the limb hanging out over the water. His hook caught in it. He gave his rod a slight flip hoping to dislodge the barb. Instead, the jerk against the line sank the hook deeper into the bark. He had to move close enough to the stream so he could grab the limb and bend it toward him. As he freed the hook, the grasshopper was knocked off. It dropped to the water, but no trout made a grab for it.

"They've seen me," Bert said to himself. "I may as well move on."

He found another pool a short distance upstream. This time he studied the trees around him before he made his cast. This one was almost perfect. The grasshopper dropped to the water close to the bank where the current had made the bottom deepest. Bert wasn't sure afterward whether or not he heard the trout splash as it grabbed the bait, but he remembered the vicious pull on the line. There was no doubt but that this fish was hooked. Bert paid out line frantically for fear the trout would break the light tackle. When the trout suddenly turned and leaped high in an attempt to shake the hook loose, Bert reeled as fast as he could. When it dived, Bert paid out line.

Bert knew this was a big trout, even larger than the other one. As he alternately paid out and reeled in, he wondered if he would be able to land this fellow. It surely was large enough to break the light line. Even if he managed to keep the fish on long enough to tire it out, the strain might snap the cord as he tried to lift it to the bank. While these thoughts were running through his mind, he was working frantically to keep the trout on his hook. He tried to keep the line tight all of the time, but not tight enough so the fish could break it. Little by little the trout's runs shortened until at last Bert had the fish close to the shore.

If he had had a dip net, Bert could have landed the trout easily. Without one he might not be able to do it. He tried lifting, but the fly rod bent dangerously indicating the strain on the tackle. Bert glanced across the pool downstream. Perhaps he could work the trout across and into the shallow water at the other end. Slowly he moved along the shore, towing the trout. The fish resisted the pull, but it was too exhausted to fight strongly. At last Bert got the prize into the shallow water at the end of the pool. The boy stepped into the water, grasped the line near the trout's mouth and dragged it safely onto the low bank.

"He'll weigh four pounds or more!" Bert exulted.

The trout was so large that it wouldn't fit into his creel. He put the head in and balanced it there with his left hand.

The temptation to try another pool was almost overpowering, but Bert resisted. Gramp had said they were to catch only enough trout for their supper. The two he had caught would easily supply them. He grinned when he remembered something that Gramp had said to him once when they were off on a fishing trip.

"There are two times when it's awfully hard to quit. One is when you haven't caught anything and you keep thinking the next cast will be it; the other is when every cast catches a fish."

This was surely one of those two times. Bert cut across from one bend of the creek to the next. The second time he reached water again, he hunted until he found the place easiest for his purpose. There, he climbed down from the bank and knelt beside the stream. He took the trout from his creel, dressed and washed them. All the time he wore a pleased smile. He'd had real luck! He put the cleaned fish into his creel and took the most direct route back to camp, anxious to show the rest.

Nancy and Jim had returned when Bert got there. Each of them had caught two trout. None was as large as the smaller one of Bert's.

"You should have brought the big one to camp and weighed it before you did the cleaning," Jim told him. "That's the largest trout I ever saw."

"I wanted to," Bert admitted, "but trout are so much better when they are dressed soon after they are caught."

"The few minutes it would have taken you to bring it to camp wouldn't have made much difference," Nancy told him.

"I'll weigh the next big one," Bert promised.

"You won't catch another one like that," Jim prophesied.

They agreed that Bert's two trout would be enough for their supper. They got the special can from the truck and put the four Nancy and Jim had caught in. Jim sank the can in the spring and Bert put a heavy rock on the lid to hold it down in the cold water. Then they joined Nancy at the campfire.

"I wonder what's keeping Gramp." Bert sounded as uneasy as he felt.

"He must have had a poorer place to fish than we did," Nancy said.

"I doubt if he is fishing," Jim said.

"What would he be doing?" Nancy demanded.

"I expect he's hiking over the pasture to see the condition of the grass and how well the cattle are doing on it," Bert answered.

Nancy glanced from Bert to Jim. She started to smile, but the smile was quickly wiped out by a look of fear.

"They really do run cattle here. We saw some of Kesterson's."

"You think he's searching for the rustlers' hide-out, don't you?" she demanded. "Maybe he found it and they caught him. We'd better go look."

"Mr. Weston is too clever to let the rustlers see him, if they are around here," Jim assured her. "There's nothing to worry about. Let's start supper. I'll cook tonight."

"Oh, no, you don't," Bert protested. "You can cook flapjacks for breakfast. I'm not going to risk having you ruin these two good trout."

Jim started to argue but when Nancy sided with Bert, he gave up. "Anyway let's get a proper fire going."

They gathered dry wood. Before they put it on the fire, they pulled away the burning sticks. They laid potatoes on the hot ground, put a layer of ashes over the potatoes, and then raked the coals back over the ashes. They put the dry wood on top of the coals. By the time the fire had burned down to new coals suitable for broiling the fish, the potatoes would be done. Nancy was just ready to broil the trout when Gramp walked into camp, empty-handed.

"Where are your fish, Mr. Weston?" she asked.

"I knew you youngsters would catch all we could eat." Gramp's eyes had a twinkle. "I took a hike over the pasture. I wanted to see if the grass here is as good as ours. I wanted to see how well the cattle do on it too, but I didn't see any cattle."

The two boys laughed at Nancy's expression. She did not know whether to believe him or not.

For the first time Gramp noticed the fish Nancy had ready for grilling.

'Who caught that big fellow?"

"Bert did," Jim said.

"Do you want to cook it, Gramp?" Bert asked. "We'd like it done just right."

"Then you should have Nancy do it," Gramp answered, but he arranged the coals and took the big fork from the girl so he could tend the fish.

In a short time Gramp announced the trout were ready. He put the big one on the platter beside the other which was done first. Bert raked the potatoes from the coals, Nancy sliced a loaf of homemade bread, and Jim got out the plates and utensils. The trout had looked as if far more than four people could eat while they were cooking, but by the time everyone had eaten his fill, there was only one small portion left. Nancy removed the bones and tossed it to Spot.

"If that isn't enough for you, you'll have to catch yourself a rabbit," Bert told the dog.

"You're always saying that to Spot," Jim said. "Why don't you give him a good meal once in a while?"

Bert didn't answer. Jim knew as well as he did that Spot was well fed. There would be enough scraps left for the dog.

"Mom sent an apple pie," Nancy announced. "We ought to eat it while it's fresh."

Bert and Jim looked at each other. Slowly they shook their heads. "I couldn't swallow another bite," Bert said. "Not even a bite of your mother's apple pie."

"Me neither," Jim agreed.

"Then I'll give it to Spot," Nancy said. "He hasn't had much."

"No! No!" the boys shouted together, jumping to their feet to stop her.

Nancy and Gramp doubled over with laughter. Bert and Jim tried to pretend they didn't understand the cause but they were soon laughing as hard as the others.

"If Bert doesn't feed Spot enough, I'll catch him a rabbit," Jim gasped between spasms of laughing, "but don't give him the apple pie."

7

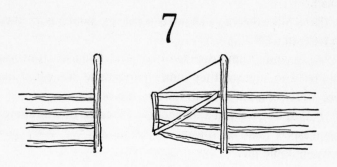

ALL OF THEM turned in early. Bert fell asleep almost as soon as he had pulled the blanket up to his chin. Once during the night Spot barked a warning. Bert raised himself up on one elbow and listened, but when the dog quieted, the boy dropped off to sleep again. Later he thought he heard a truck off in the distance, but he didn't fully awaken, and next morning he wasn't quite sure that he hadn't dreamed of hearing the truck.

Jim was up and busily preparing breakfast when the others came to the fire. He had the four trout that he and Nancy had caught broiling on a grate, the steaming coffee pot beside the fire, and flapjacks browning on the griddle.

"I was going to catch more trout for your breakfast," he told them with a grin, "but I decided you'd rather have more of these delicious flapjacks."

"If you'd do more cooking and less bragging, we'd get our breakfast," Bert complained.

Jim quickly silenced the complaint. He put one of the

browned trout and three flapjacks on a plate and handed it to his friend.

"How are we going to keep our fish so we can take some home with us?" Nancy asked.

"At the end of every hour clean whatever you have caught," Gramp told her. "Wrap the fish in wet watercress. They'll be fresh when you get back to camp."

"I have to remember that seven is the limit," Jim said solemnly. "I don't want to have a game warden arrest me."

"You'll be lucky to catch any," Bert scoffed.

Jim didn't bother to answer that gibe. He turned to Gramp and asked, "Will it be all right if we fish upstream this morning?"

"Let's save that for the afternoon," Gramp answered after a moment's hesitation. "I won't fish this morning. I'll get some of our gear packed."

Nancy, Jim, and Bert caught a supply of grasshoppers before they went their ways. When Nancy left the two boys to go to the stream, Spot followed her. Bert and Jim walked downstream until they were out of sight of Nancy. Here they stopped and dropped to the ground as if they had agreed to this plan before they left camp.

"Your grandfather is going to look upstream for the rustlers' hiding place," Jim said.

Bert nodded. "That's the reason he didn't want us to fish there this morning."

"We could circle back that way. We might help him find them."

Bert gave his friend a surprised look. He had been thinking that as soon as he left Jim, he would do just that—circle back and either join his grandfather or search alone in the same direction. Now that Jim had proposed that plan, he saw it wasn't a very good one.

"We'd probably just interfere with what Gramp's doing," he said.

"I suppose," Jim agreed reluctantly.

The boys were quiet for a few minutes, each going over in his own mind various possibilities as to where the rustlers might have their hiding place. Bert broke the silence.

"You remember from the very first raid the rustlers made at the Henderson place, everyone has been sure that someone in the neighborhood has to be in with them?"

Jim nodded.

"Well, I've been thinking, that first morning, at branding time, Speck didn't come to help. Bill said he was in town too late the night before. He could have been with the rustlers or spotting a place to load the next bunch they took."

"Gosh, that's right," Jim exclaimed jumping to his feet. "That's a good clue. Let's get back to camp before your grandfather leaves and tell him so he can get word to the sheriff."

Jim headed toward camp, but by the time Bert had scrambled to his feet to go with him, Jim turned back.

"Bill missed a day of branding too. No one would suspect Henderson's foreman of being in with rustlers."

"That's right. I suppose that if the sheriff looked around other ranches, he'd find more hands who were away from them until late at night."

"I guess we're not as good detectives as we thought," Jim admitted ruefully. "We might as well do some fishing."

He broke off a couple of blades of grass and fitted them in his hand. He held them out to Bert, but Bert waved them away.

"I fished the good holes yesterday," he said. "You go down there today and I'll fish here."

As soon as Jim started on downstream, Bert went to the creek. He made his way carefully along until he found a good place. Fitting a grasshopper to his hook, he cast it with care. The grasshopper lit lightly on the water, but there was no least ripple of a trout rising to the bait. Bert drew his line in and made another cast. Nothing happened. It was then that he realized he was standing so that the sun cast his shadow onto the water. He had frightened any fish away.

He searched downstream until he came on another pool. This time he made sure that the sun was shining in his face and his shadow falling behind him before he made his cast. The first careful fling was answered by a great ripple breaking upward and action on the line. It took several minutes for him to play the trout out and land it. It wasn't as large as those he had caught yesterday, but it was a fine rainbow.

At the next pool he hooked a big trout, but it made an unexpected dive and snapped his line. He put on a new hook and dropped it in neatly several times but without result. He fished Winding Creek until he had landed three trout. Then he decided he would quit. If it turned out that there was good fishing upstream, he would be free to catch four more before he had his limit.

Bert cleaned his trout and returned to camp. As he had expected, Gramp wasn't there. His grandfather had taken down Nancy's small tent and stowed it in the truck, but the big tent was still standing. He had not put much of the gear away after all. Well, it was as they had thought, just an excuse.

Bert put his fish into the pail and sank it to the bottom of the spring. He thought of hiking upstream, but decided against it. As he had told Jim, any interference might spoil Gramp's plan. Instead, he started packing the camp gear and putting it on the truck. He was still working at that task when Nancy returned to camp with three fine trout. He helped her put them into the pail with the others.

"Gramp and Jim will bring in all we can eat for one meal," he said.

Bert and Nancy gathered dry wood and started the cook fire. While they waited for the others, they tidied up the camping place and chatted. It was noon when Gramp returned to camp from the west and Jim from the east. Gramp was empty-handed, but Jim was carrying a trout too large to fit into his creel.

"I didn't clean this one," Jim explained as he dashed into camp. "I want to weigh it."

"It's as big or bigger than the one I caught," Bert told his friend.

The others watched as he weighed the trout. "Four pounds and a half," Jim exulted, studying the scales. "The rest of you check what I say. I don't want to be accused of telling fish stories when I give out the details about this one."

In turn Gramp, Nancy, and Bert looked at the scales.

"That one will be enough for our meal," Gramp said. "You dress it, Jim, while I get the other things ready."

Gramp decided there were not enough embers in the fire Bert and Nancy had started, so he had them get more dry wood. Before he added the fresh fuel, he took some yams and carrots from the supplies they had brought. He used a stick to work the vegetables down into the ashes.

By the time the fire had burned down to embers, Jim had his trout ready for the grill. While they waited for the fish, Jim told of his struggle to land it. After he finished there was silence, broken only by the sizzling of the trout on the grill. Bert turned to his grandfather.

"I don't suppose you found any sign of the rustlers' hide-out?" he asked.

Gramp gave him a surprised look and then he began to laugh.

"I might have known I wasn't fooling you youngsters," he said ruefully. "I didn't expect to find it along this stream, but I did think it could be nearby, or that at least I might find a trail leading to it."

"Maybe their hide-out is across the state line," Jim suggested. "That can't be more than five miles north of here."

"It could be," Gramp agreed, "but it isn't likely. If they took stolen goods across a state line, the FBI could be called in."

"But they undoubtedly haul the cattle across state lines when they sell them," Bert pointed out.

"At least I didn't find any trace of anything," Gramp answered. "I'm convinced their hide-out isn't in this neighborhood. This afternoon I am going to fish and you may try your luck anywhere along the stream that you choose."

"I'm going back downstream where the big ones are," Jim announced quickly.

"I'm going to fish upstream," Nancy decided. "I think I can catch some big ones up there."

"I'll fish above whatever place Nancy chooses," Bert said. "There may be even better trout up there than there is downstream."

"I'll fish near Jim," Gramp told them. "But right now let's eat. Everything is ready."

This time Bert and Jim remembered the apple pie. They left a larger portion of trout for Spot so that they would have room for pie.

"Next time we go on a fishing trip, we want you to do all the cooking, Mr. Weston," Nancy said seriously. "This is the best meal I've ever eaten."

"Gramp knows how to broil trout," Bert agreed, "but your mother's apple pie added that little extra that made the meal complete."

"Little extra," Jim snorted. "I noticed you took the biggest piece of pie on the plate."

"The biggest one after you selected yours," Bert reminded him with a laugh.

Bert and Nancy left camp together. Instead of walking along the stream, they took a straight course and avoided the windings of the creek. Nancy selected a place about a mile from camp to make her first try. She would follow the stream back. She ought to have the five fish she wanted long before she reached the truck.

"I'll take Spot with me this time," Bert offered. "He doesn't seem to bring you good luck."

"Oh, no," Nancy answered in haste. "I like to have him with me."

Spot understood what had been said all right. He looked up and wagged his tail at Bert, but when Nancy started toward the bank of the stream, he followed her.

Bert watched them off, eyes filled with pride. There was a smart dog.

The valley through which the stream ran was much narrower here. Back where they had pitched their camp, there was a wide level stretch on both sides of the stream. As Bert and Nancy had walked upstream, they found that the amount of level land grew less and less. Steep inclines closed in and the valley became narrower and narrower. After he left Nancy, Bert found the valley still narrowing until it was little more than a canyon. Sometimes the creek ran so close to one of the walls that he had to cross to the other side.

Bert went on until he found a place where the north bank sloped enough so that he could climb it. He made his way to the top. From there he could see another valley to the north and beyond it other rows of trees that meant there were still more valleys beyond. The plan that had been half formed in his mind when he decided to fish upstream, now became definite. Gramp certainly hadn't had time to explore all of those valleys. There would be trout streams in some without doubt. Bert thought this would give him a chance to look for the rustlers' hide-out and at the same time fish in a different stream. He might catch another big trout.

There were so many trees along the slope ahead of him that Bert could not see whether or not there was a stream in this next valley. It didn't really matter. If there wasn't a trout stream in this valley, there probably would be in the next and he had all afternoon to catch five trout. He walked along the crest of the hill watching for a place where the slope was gentle enough so that he could go down without difficulty. As he made his way, he watched for cattle or horse tracks, although he didn't really expect to find signs of the rustlers here. Gramp would have searched this first valley carefully.

When he got to the bottom of the hill, Bert found that there was a small stream flowing through this valley. There were no pools near him, though he was quite sure that if he should follow along the bank he would find some. But he was too interested in exploring to take the time. He went up the hill on the north side. From the top, he saw that the next valley did not extend nearly as far to the west as the one he had just left or the next one north of it.

Bert hesitated, trying to decide what he should do. He thought it probably would be a waste of time to explore the valley just ahead. Undoubtedly Gramp had studied it thoroughly. It might even be a waste of time to examine the valley on the other side of that one. Bert took another look toward the second valley. As far as he could see the clusters of trees extended to the west. Evidently that valley stretched farther in that direction than any of its neighbors. It might be that Gramp hadn't explored far enough in that direction.

Bert made a quick check on the sun. There was plenty of daylight left. Again he glanced to the northwest. He could take a slanting course that would avoid the canyon just ahead. That would save the time he would otherwise lose climbing up and down hills. He decided he'd make a real survey of that second valley. If he found time getting short, afterward he would go directly back to camp. There would be other times for fishing. He set off at a rapid pace.

The canyon that he was avoiding proved to extend farther than Bert had first judged. He had to walk a mile or more before he could turn toward the valley he wanted to explore. Fortunately the high land between was almost level, so he could maintain his rapid pace.

The grass in this area was thick and so tall that it reached almost to his knees. It wouldn't be this tall if cattle had been grazing over it. Ahead of him Bert noticed a pair of tracks marked out in bent grass. As he came nearer, he saw that the tracks were such marks as are left by a heavy vehicle. A truck had been driven across here. Bert hesitated. If a rancher had been through, it must mean that he had cattle in the valley ahead. If a rancher had cattle there, the rustlers wouldn't be using it for a hide-out. But Bert was half-way to the valley which was his objective. He had come this far, he might as well go the rest of the distance and take a look. He had gone on only a short bit more when he found another set of truck tracks. A little farther on he found another set, and beyond them still another.

"That's clever," he said to himself. "This way no easy-to-follow trail is made."

He realized now that he had probably crossed other places where the truck had been driven without noticing them. The grass would have straightened up in a few days and of the few people who came here who would have noticed? For the first time Bert was afraid. Whoever had driven that truck back and forth had intended to hide his tracks. For the first time Bert realized that he had come a long way from camp and was far from any possible help. At the same moment he also realized that standing here on the ridge he could be seen a long way. He dropped to his hands and knees; the grass almost hid him.

When Bert raised his head and gazed toward the canyon beyond, he knew he couldn't crawl that far on his hands and knees. If he was to take a look into that canyon, he would have to stand up and walk there. He hesitated only a moment. He had come too far to give up now. He got to his feet, crouched as low as he could, and hurried forward. He felt much safer when he was near enough that trees and shrubs offered some concealment.

As soon as he reached the edge of the canyon, Bert began to search for a place where the trees were far enough apart so that he could get a look down into the valley. It took him only a little time to find such a place. He saw a few cattle grazing in the valley. From where he was they looked as if they were yearlings, but the distance was too great for him to be sure. He began cautiously descending to get closer. He had gone only a few steps down the slope when the bawling of a calf stopped him. It was the kind of high-pitched frightened bawl that a calf gives when it's being branded.

Bert crouched down and listened. The second bawl convinced him he was right. After all, he'd been hearing a whole lot of that sound the last few days. He knew the branding might well be in progress with a regular crew. Nevertheless, the frightened bawl of still another calf sent a chill along his spine.

There was too much danger that he might be seen here, so Bert moved to a better hiding place. From this new vantage point, he could see only a little of the valley below. The location from which the bawling of the calves had come was completely out of sight, farther up the canyon to the west. If he was to find out for sure what was going on, he had to get closer. Resolutely Bert set out in the direction of the sounds.

He had gone only a short distance before he changed his mind about the best way to approach the branding crew. If those doing the branding were the rustlers they might have someone watching the valley. It would be safer to cross over and go to the top of the crest on the other side. The creek at the foot of the hill was so narrow that he easily stepped across it. He made his way through the screening trees to the heights on the north side of the valley.

Bert wished that he had brought Spot with him. He wouldn't have felt so alone if the smart dog with his alert senses had been with him. Uneasily he realized it had been a long time since he heard a calf bawl. From his place at the top of the rise he couldn't see the branding crew. There were too many trees along the hillside. He would have to get still closer.

Carefully he worked his way along toward the position he sought. Instead of following the crest he went a few steps back down so that there would be less chance that he would be seen by any possible watcher. He moved along the slope until he reached a place where he could see the branding crew working.

Bert's first glimpse convinced him he had found the rustlers' hide-out. A small pole corral had been set up in the middle of the valley. A short distance farther west a big truck, the kind used for hauling cattle long distances, was parked. Near the corral was a small fire. Undoubtedly it was used for heating the branding irons. Four men were driving a small herd of yearlings toward the corral. The men were too far away for Bert to make out their features, but something about one of them was familiar.

The men were having considerable trouble moving the cattle toward the corral. They were accustomed to doing this kind of work on horseback. On foot they had to dart from place to place to keep some of the calves from break-ing away from the herd. As the men hurried back and forth trying to drive the cattle, Bert watched the one who seemed familiar. The longer he watched the man, the more certain he became this was someone he knew. "It might be Speck," he said to himself, remembering the morning Speck hadn't been able to help with the branding because he had been out all night.

If the man proved to be Speck, it would explain why the rustlers had been so successful. Speck knew the country around the Henderson ranch. He had worked for Henderson longer than any other man in the crew, with the exception of Bill Stewart. Speck would know where cattle could be loaded on all the surrounding ranches and he would know about that rough land on the Carter place.

The four men at last drove the last of the calves into the corral and closed the makeshift gate behind them. One and all they dropped to the ground to rest.

As the men loafed near the corral, apparently in no hurry to resume work, Bert began to fidget. If Gramp and Nancy and Jim caught their limit of trout quickly and returned to camp, they would begin to worry. They might send Spot to look for him. They would know that he would understand Spot was sent to fetch him because it was time for him to return to camp. He could almost see his dog racing across the valley, barking triumphantly as he dashed straight to his master's hiding place. He knew the rustlers, if they were rustlers, would be able to interpret such actions. They would jump up, fan out, surround and capture him in no time.

Bert pushed those thoughts out of his mind. He needed to decide what to do. He could return to camp and tell Gramp what he had seen. Gramp might come to investigate, but that would be a waste of time. Bert might as well do the investigating while he was here.

At last the men he watched began to stir about. One of them put wood on the fire. Another walked toward the truck. Bert knew now he had to get closer to that corral. From where he was hiding, he couldn't make out the men's features. More important, he wouldn't know whether the men were branding animals that had never been branded before or if they were putting new brands over old ones.

Cautiously the boy moved nearer the top of the hill. He looked at the slope around and above him to make sure there was no sentry on his side of the valley. Next he turned and studied the hillside to the south. If there was a watcher, he would be on that side of the camp. Bert let his glance travel slowly up to a point just across. Then he turned his head, studying the top of the hill from the point across from him and going to the west. At a position directly above the corral he thought he saw a movement. He watched the spot intently. Slowly a figure rose from behind a shrub and looked down into the valley. Bert gave a gasp of dismay. Even from this distance he knew it was Nancy on the other hillside!

"Get down! Get down!" He thought the words so desperately that he wasn't sure he hadn't shouted them. Nancy ducked. Bert took a quick look at the rustlers to see if they were coming toward him. But the rustlers were still going about their tasks around the branding fire. The one who had gone to the truck was back at the fire and was handing a couple of irons to the man Bert had decided must be Speck. Bert's heart seemed to choke him as he saw that one of the men was looking toward the top of the hill. Bert was able to breathe normally again when the man turned lazily and walked over to another of the crew. The two of them left their companion and walked west up the valley.

For a short time Bert watched the two men. He wondered what they could be doing. The four of them had had so much trouble bringing in a herd that it didn't seem likely only two were going to try to drive more cattle to the corral. Bert turned his attention from the two men to the hillside between him and the corral. He had to get nearer and he had to do it before Nancy herself rashly crept closer. He saw that if he was careful, he could creep from shrub to shrub and still stay concealed. He started at once.

Bert paused only occasionally to make sure the men hadn't seen him. The two who had left the campfire were out of sight. The two at the campfire seemed merely to be waiting for the branding irons to heat. The nearer he came to the corral, the more carefully Bert moved. At last he reached a place only a few yards from the fire. It was an ideal place for concealment. The low branches of the trees made a good screen between him and the men, and there was a leafy shrub that made his hiding place even more secure.

Bert squirmed around until he was in a position to watch the men but there was little danger that they could see him. He had just settled himself when one of the men beside the fire got to his feet and turned enough for Bert to see his face. The boy gave a tremendous sigh of relief. The man was Bill Stewart, Henderson's foreman. These weren't rustlers. They were a branding crew from a neighboring ranch. Evidently Mr. Henderson had bought a whole herd of yearlings and sent his men up here to brand them.

Bert started to get to his feet to go to the corral and speak to Bill. He stopped before he had raised himself off the ground. The feeling of relief he had had at the sight of Bill turned to a mixture of fear and anger that held him chained where he was. The man with Bill wasn't one of Henderson's men, nor were the two who had disappeared. Bill was the only one who had looked familiar when he first sighted them. Bill was one of the rustlers!

At first it was almost impossible to believe, but the proof was all here. The men had talked about the many nights Bill spent in town. He hadn't been in town. He had been helping the rustlers. He was the one who knew all the possible loading places. He was the one who could handle branding irons so skillfully that every rancher wanted him. He would be the one who could put a new brand over an old one in such a way that it wouldn't be noticed.

Bill and his companion went toward the corral. Bert watched to see how two men would throw a yearling calf and one hold it still enough so that the other could brand it. But the men did no throwing. The corral had been built with a narrow passage at one corner. The passage was barely wide enough to allow one calf through at a time. Bill and his companion crowded a calf into the aisle. Bill's helper put a pole from one side of the aisle to the other in such a way that it wedged the calf tightly. Bill took one of the hot irons from the fire. He returned to the corral, dropped to one knee, shoved the hot iron between two of the poles, and held it against the animal's shoulder for a moment. There came a frightened bawl, but the calf was unable to move. As soon as Bill withdrew the iron, the other man opened the gate in front and the calf scampered away. The man reclosed the gate, pulled the pole back and they were ready to put another calf into the branding cage.

Bert turned his attention from the corral to look toward Nancy's hiding place. He had to put his hand over his mouth to keep from shouting. Nancy had moved several steps down the hill from her first hiding place. Now she was standing in plain sight trying to hold Spot. Spot gave a sharp warning bark, but Nancy didn't understand. The next moment the two men who had left the corral earlier grabbed her.

If Nancy screamed, her scream wasn't loud enough for Bert to hear it. One of the men let go of Nancy and stepped back. Bert saw him pulling a revolver from a holster under his jacket. Nancy had quit struggling, she was looking down, and Bert was sure she was saying something to Spot. The man now had his revolver out and was taking aim. Bert knew from the way the man was slowly raising his arm that he was taking aim at Spot and that the dog was running away. As though he had heard her, Bert knew that Nancy had ordered Spot to go for help. How Spot must have wanted to throw himself at Nancy's captors instead of obeying her orders!

Bert felt tears stinging against his eyelids. Spot wouldn't have a chance! He would start to obey, but he would stop to look back. He would be asking Nancy to change her mind and let him handle these men the way they ought to be handled. While he stopped to look back, he would be a perfect target.

But the man didn't fire. Evidently the other said something to stop him. Slowly the man put his gun back into the holster. He stepped to one side of Nancy and grabbed her arm. The other man took her other arm. Together they brought her toward the corral.

Bert looked to see what the two men at the corral were doing. They were merely standing there waiting for the others. Bert moved his head to look for some tree limb that would serve as a club if he had to rush the four men. There was one that looked as if it would do, only a few feet to his left. Slowly he crept toward it. He was reaching his hand out to grasp it when he heard a stealthy movement in the brush behind. There must have been a lookout on the other hill after all. From the sounds he knew the lookout was coming straight toward him. He would be caught between that one and the four men at the corral. Bert grasped the club, got to a crouching position, and turned to face this new danger.

His relief was so great he could hardly keep from shouting. Spot was trotting toward him!

8

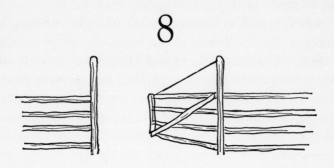

CAREFULLY BERT dropped to his hands and knees. As Spot crowded to his side, the boy turned to look at the men. The two at the corral were still waiting for the other two to bring Nancy there. They were so intent upon their approach that it was plain they hadn't heard Bert's sudden movement. Bert turned to Spot.

"Get Gramp," he whispered urgently. "Get Gramp."

Spot was staring at the men bringing Nancy to the corral. The hair on the scruff of his neck was standing erect and there was a low menacing growl deep in his throat.

"Shhh," Bert warned and again ordered, "Get Gramp."

Spot was so intent on the men that he seemed not to hear. For an agonizing moment Bert was afraid the dog was going to disobey him and rush at the men. He knew this time the armed man wouldn't hesitate. He would draw his gun and shoot Spot before the dog could get to him. Bert put his hand on Spot's neck and pulled the dog's head close to him. "Get Gramp," he ordered.

With obvious reluctance Spot backed away from his master. Suddenly he turned and dashed down the valley.

Bert went back to watching the rustlers. The two bringing Nancy to the corral were momentarily out of sight behind a clump of brush. While he waited for them to reappear, Bert looked about his hiding place to find the best way to leave it if he had to attack the men. He saw that by taking two steps to his left, he would be able to dash out without being hampered by as many low branches as he would be if he went straight from where he was hiding.

The two outlaws and Nancy were now almost at the fire. Bill took a step forward to meet them. "What are you doing here, Nancy?" he demanded.

"I was fishing until I caught my limit," Nancy answered. "Then I decided to look around. When I got to the top of the hill, I saw you branding. I was watching you when these two characters grabbed me. I didn't know Mr. Henderson had bought a herd of cattle over here."

"Clever girl," Bert said to himself. "The rustlers might just fall for that."

Bert saw the four men look at one another. He knew that at least some of them were thinking this might be an easy way out of the difficulty. If Nancy thought they were branding for Mr. Henderson, they could let her go.

"She was watchin' mighty close and bein' mighty careful that no one down here saw her when me and Slim grabbed her," said one of the men who had brought Nancy down the hill.

"She sure was," Slim agreed. "If Curly had let me, I would have shot her dog. He might lead someone here."

"You're a fool," Curly growled. "We'd best get rid of her. That will leave us a little extra time to clear out."

The outlaw had spoken so matter-of-factly that at first Bert wondered if he meant what he seemed to be saying. He saw by the looks on the faces of the other men that Curly did mean it.

"None of that, Curly," Bill protested. "Rustling is one thing; murder is another."

"You're carrying a gun," Curly answered in a reasonable tone. "You'd use it if you thought it necessary."

"There must be some other way," the outlaw who hadn't yet spoken suggested.

"You tell us the other way, Pete," Curly sneered.

"Why sure," Pete answered, "and it will give us more time than knocking her in the head would. We can tie her and leave her here. It'll take them a long time to find her."

"Too chancey," Curly said. "We'll get rid of her along the road. Let's get things ready so we can load. It's just possible that they'll come this way looking for her."

"They wouldn't if you'd have let me shoot that dog," Slim told him.

"Shooting to scare kids off while we loaded Bill's horse was one thing," Curly snapped, "but shooting here would be different. When neither the dog nor the girl came back, someone would remember hearing a shot in this direction. They'd come straight here."

"But the dog might lead them here," Slim protested.

"You've read too many dog stories," Curly answered.

"We'd better get to work," Bill reminded them.

Curly ordered Slim and Pete to tie Nancy's hands and feet.

104

As soon as they finished, the four men became extremely busy. Pete hurried to the truck as the others went to the corral. By the time the three at the corral had the first calf branded, Pete backed the big truck up to the aisle gate. He dropped the tailgate and put boards beside it to make a chute. Now the freshly branded calves were driven up the chute into the truck.

With all four of them intent at the job, the calves were quickly worked over and loaded into the truck.

"We'll drive the others in and load them right away," Curly decided.

Bert's hopes soared as the men turned to go up the valley. As soon as they were out of sight, he would cut Nancy's bonds. They'd make it back to camp by the time the rustlers came in with the calves and discovered that Nancy was gone. A telephone call over party lines to alert the neighborhood and this time the rustlers would be caught! But his hopes were dashed as quickly as they had risen. Curly had stopped. Now he spoke to Pete. "You go back and put the rest of the fuel in the truck tank."

"O.K."

"You'd just as well get supper too," Curly called. "Keep a sharp watch. We don't want anyone wandering unexpectedly down here."

Pete returned to the truck and the others were soon out of sight. Pete took the two five-gallon cans beside the truck and emptied them into the truck's fuel tank. Then he climbed up onto the top of the cab. Slowly he turned around looking intently at the hillsides and the valley. When he climbed down he went to the front of the machine and lifted the hood.

He put his feet on the bumper and leaned far under the hood examining something. Bert knew this was the best chance he would have. He grabbed the club, got to his feet, and tensed himself to rush across the open space to the truck. Before Bert could start, Pete pulled his head back, stepped to the ground, and slammed the hood down. The chance was gone.

Pete tossed more wood on the fire. He took two forked sticks and stuck them into the ground at opposite sides of the fire. He got a large black kettle, thrust a stick through the bail, put water in the kettle, and swung it over the fire by putting one end of the stick on the notched sticks. He took a chunk of meat from the box of supplies. This he cut into small pieces and dropped them into the kettle of water. Next he got a black coffee pot, rinsed it out carelessly, put water and coffee in it and set it beside the fire. Next he got potatoes and onions which he peeled and put on a large plate.

"What are you going to do with me?" Nancy asked him.

"That's up to Curly. He's the boss."

"You must have something to say about what's done," Nancy insisted.

"I'd be in favor of hiding you back there in the trees where it would be hard to find you," Pete answered.

"Not tied like this!"

"What else can we do?" Pete asked reasonably. "Turn you loose so you can run to your friends and call the sheriff?"

"What if I promised to stay here until morning?" Nancy asked.

"I might believe you," Pete answered, "but Curly wouldn't. He's a mistrusting man."

"If you don't leave me here, what will you do with me?"

"I don't know," Pete answered uneasily. "Now shut up. I have things to do."

In spite of his fear Bert smiled to himself. Nancy was stirring up doubts in Pete's mind. Probably the man had been trying to tell himself that Curly would try to find some easy way to get the girl out of the way long enough for the rustlers to make their getaway. But her questions had made Pete face the fact that Curly intended murder. Bert gave a little shuddering gasp. He hadn't really faced that fact before either, but now he had to. If no one stopped him, Curly would put Nancy out of the way so that she could never tell what she had seen. Bert took a firmer grip on his club. Somehow he would have to stop Curly.

The shouts of the men driving the calves toward the corral became audible. It seemed impossible for men to drive cattle without shouting at them. The rustlers were holding their voices down, but they were continually calling out angrily.

Pete dropped the plate of vegetables into the kettle over the fire. Then he trotted over to the corral to be ready to head off any calves that tried to escape. Bert laid his club on the ground, took his knife from his pocket, and opened it. If some of the calves escaped the herders, he would have a chance to dash out, cut Nancy's ropes, and lead her to safety. He felt a bit better for having such a plan because he knew it had a far better chance for success than a single-handed attack against the armed rustlers. He waited tensely for one or more of the calves to act up, giving him an opportunity in the confusion.

The first calf to approach the gate did try to make a break, but Pete stepped out and turned it back. The others followed the leader into the corral. In a few minutes it was all over.

As soon as the gate swung shut behind the last calf, Pete dashed to the cooking fire. He took a long-handled fork, speared a chunk of meat, and looked at it. He shook the piece of meat off the tines of the fork and back into the kettle.

"Come on," Curly called impatiently. "Let's get these calves loaded."

"I was just making sure of our meal," Pete answered, turning back toward the others.

Bert watched the rustlers anxiously. If all of them climbed into the corral, he might have a chance to free Nancy. If her legs were not tied so tight that her feet were numb, they would need only a little head start to get away. But only three of the men climbed in. Curly stayed on the outside. Part of the time he helped prod the calves down the narrow aisle and up the chute into the truck. At other times he climbed up onto the top rail of the corral and looked about the countryside to make sure they weren't going to be surprised by someone approaching the camp. He looked toward Nancy so often that Bert had no chance to try out his plan.

As soon as all the calves were loaded, the tail gate was locked into place. Pete went to the fire and again tested the meat. "It ain't quite done," he announced.

Curly nodded unconcernedly. "Pour us cups of that coffee," he ordered.

Pete picked up four tin cups from where they had been tossed to the ground. He flipped the dregs out of them, rinsed them sketchily and filled them with coffee.

"What are we going to do with that girl?" Bill asked as he took one of the cups of coffee.

"We can take her in the truck," Slim suggested. "We could put her out along that long stretch where there ain't no houses. We'd be safely out of the country before she could give the alarm."

"Suppose a car comes along and picks her up?" Curly demanded.

"We never have met any cars on that strip," Pete pointed out.

"You're a bunch of softies," Curly sneered. "If we get rid of her permanently, we don't take any chances."

"That's out," Bill said, speaking with sudden firmness and the others nodded.

Curly shrugged. "We'll probably be sorry. How's the food coming, Pete?"

Pete jabbed a piece of meat with the fork. "Come and git it," he called.

The men picked up plates and tin forks. Pete ladled out generous helpings of the stew. The tantalizing smell made Bert remember it had been a long time since he had eaten. He glanced toward the sun dropping behind the western hills. Maybe Gramp hadn't understood why Spot had gone to camp. For the first time Bert realized that Gramp would think Nancy had sent Spot to camp for help. He would waste a lot of time looking along the creek for her.

With all his heart Bert wished he had kept Spot beside

him. He might have been able to take the rustlers by surprise and the dog would have backed him up. Somehow they would have won enough time to free Nancy and escape. His gloomy thoughts were interrupted by the talk at the campfire.

"How soon can we start?" Bill asked.

Curly glanced to the west. "We'd better wait another hour," he decided. "Our truck will be less noticeable after dark when only headlights stand out."

Bert shivered. One more hour! He put the knife back into his pocket and again picked up the club. If help didn't come, he would have to attack the gang single-handed. Curly's apparent giving in to the demands of the gang about Nancy hadn't fooled him. He knew Curly would find an opportunity to push Nancy from the truck sometime when it was speeding over a deserted stretch of road. The rustler had no intention of leaving her alive to give her information to the sheriff.

The men loaded their belongings onto the truck and then stood about uneasily.

"Here we are like sitting ducks," Slim complained. "If they come looking for the girl, they'll stumble right onto us."

"Quit beefing," Curly snapped. "We can handle an old man and a couple of boys."

Bert's spirits hit a new low. There was not much the men did not know. What chance was there against them?

Pete climbed into the engine cab and slid behind the wheel. Slim walked around to the other side of the truck. Even Bill got up and walked restlessly around. Only Curly seemed to be at ease.

110

"Better look around to make sure you haven't left anything," Curly called at last. "We'll be leaving in five minutes."

Again Bert tensed himself. This would be his only chance. He had to take it. If all four men came to this side of the truck, he would leap out and charge them with the club. There was a possibility that he could take them completely by surprise and knock all of them out. He watched Pete anxiously. If the driver stayed in the cab, there was no chance that Bert's plan would work. Bert saw Pete feel in his pockets. Slowly he opened the door and climbed down.

Slim and Bill had returned to Curly's side. Pete searched near the fire, leaned over, picked something up, and put it in his pocket. He came toward the others. Bert set himself. As soon as Pete took two more steps, it would be time to charge. Before the man took the second of those two steps, there was the sound of rapid movement in the brush on the other side of the creek. The four men whirled in that direction. Bert turned to look too. He could hardly believe what he saw. Spot came romping out of the underbrush carrying an old cap in his mouth.

Before the men had decided what to do Spot had raced across the clearing and under the limbs of the tree where Bert was hiding. He dropped the cap at his master's feet and gave an excited bark. Bert stood up. There was no point in trying to hide now. How could Spot be so stupid when he had been so smart before? Bert stepped out of his hiding place and the four men started toward him. Curly was reaching for his gun.

"Stop where you are and get your hands up," ordered a voice from the shrubs behind the rustlers.

The men stopped as though all four had been caught by a rope jerked tight. Slowly they raised their hands.

"Face this way," the voice went on and now Bert knew it for the voice of Sheriff Cameron.

9

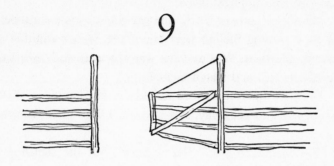

As BILL, CURLY, PETE AND SLIM obeyed the sheriff's order, Bert advanced so he could see better in the direction they were facing. Sheriff Cameron and two deputies had stepped out into the clearing. Each had a rifle aimed at the rustlers. Gramp and Jim were a few steps behind the sheriff and his men. Bert gave a shuddering sigh of relief. Nancy was safe. He reached down and stroked his dog's ears affectionately. How could he have doubted him! Spot had done just what he was supposed to do. By running directly to Bert he had distracted the outlaws long enough for the sheriff and his men to get the drop on them. The whole gang had been captured without a shot being fired!

"Run, you guys!" Curly shouted suddenly. "They won't shoot you."

Without pausing to see whether or not the others followed, Curly himself turned and ran. Bert ducked and closed his eyes as the sheriff fired, but even before his eyes shut, he saw that the sheriff had aimed high over Curly's head.

"That's a warning," Sheriff Cameron called grimly. "I'll get you with the next one."

By way of answer Curly dodged behind some shrubbery. With a sinking feeling Bert heard the rustler running off among the trees. Was that the way it was to end? Must the ranchers wait and watch again?

Sheriff Cameron glanced quickly at his deputies. "If any of these try to get away, shoot to hit. I'll go after the other one."

"He'll ambush you," Bert warned, but the sheriff paid no attention.

Bert watched as Sheriff Cameron vanished behind the first shrub at the edge of the trees. Although the valley was still light, it was almost dark among the trees. It would be easy for Curly to hide and shoot the sheriff from ambush. Bert knew the rustler was capable of it. Curly would try anything to escape. There was only one thing to do. He turned to Spot. "Get him," he ordered.

Spot dashed off the same way the sheriff had gone and Bert raced after him. The boy was panting hard by the time he caught up with the sheriff. Spot was now well in front.

"Keep back," Sheriff Cameron ordered.

Ahead of them Spot gave an angry snarl. There was a crash as someone fell in the underbrush. The sounds were not so far off after all. The crash was followed by a cry of terror.

Bert was a step behind the sheriff when they reached the center of activities. The sight was worth their effort. Curly was prone on the ground. He was thrashing about and trying to kick off the dog that had him by one ankle.

"Stop him! Stop him before he kills me!" Curly shouted.

"Call your dog off, Bert," Sheriff Cameron ordered.

"That man has a gun," Bert protested. "If Spot lets him go, he'll shoot at us."

"He knocked the gun out of my hand when he tripped me. Call him off before he tears my foot off." Real terror was evident in the man's voice.

"I have him covered," the sheriff said, "and he knows he'd better not try anything more. Call the dog off, Bert."

"Let him go, Spot," his master ordered.

Spot let go. He backed off a step, but stayed in a crouch, ready to spring if Curly tried to get up. The rustler made to reach a hand toward his injured leg, but thought better of it with the sheriff's gun pointed at him.

"Get me to a doctor," Curly pleaded. "That mad dog bit me."

"See if you can find his gun, Bert," the sheriff ordered.

Bert went down on hands and knees. He felt around in the underbrush until his hand touched the gun. He picked it up and carried it to the sheriff.

"Set the safety," Sheriff Cameron ordered, "and then drop it into my pocket."

Bert did as the officer ordered. Sheriff Cameron continued to keep his gun pointed at Curly. Now he motioned to the outlaw. "Get to your feet."

"Take me to a doctor, quick," Curly whimpered as he rose awkwardly. "I tell you that dog is mad."

"You get back to the others," the sheriff answered. "If that dog is mad, he's the first obedient mad dog I ever saw."

Curly limped toward the truck. The sheriff followed, his

gun at the ready. Bert and Spot followed the officer. By the time they reached the truck, Nancy's bonds had been cut. She was still working to restore circulation to her hands. The three rustlers were standing with their hands tied behind them.

"Can you drive that cattle truck, Mr. Weston?" Sheriff Cameron asked.

"Yes."

"You and the youngsters ride in it. We'll walk these fellows to the car. I'll take them to the Barber place. You follow."

"Let me ride in the truck," Curly begged. "I'll bleed to death walking to the car."

"That'll be one way of keeping out of prison," the sheriff answered grimly. "Get going."

The rustlers trudged off, the sheriff and his deputies following them with drawn guns. Gramp let them get several paces ahead before he started the truck. He let the truck creep along behind the procession, until they reached the place where the sheriff had left his car. Gramp stopped the truck beside the car. He waited while the sheriff bandaged Curly's leg and loaded the rustlers into the car.

"You lead the way to the Barber place," the sheriff ordered.

All the way in, Bert watched the rear view mirror on his side of the truck. Spot remained tense and alert, ready for anything. Afraid that somehow Curly would find a way to escape, neither one relaxed. The car stayed close behind the truck. When they stopped in front of the Barber house, Bert saw that all of the rustlers were safely in the car.

The sheriff arranged for Mr. Barber to take Gramp, Nancy, and the two boys back to their camping place. He and his deputies would wait until Mr. Barber returned. Then they would put two of the outlaws in each car and take them to jail. It would be safer to separate the rustlers.

"We won't take time to cook a meal," Gramp told the young people when they reached the campsite. "Mrs. Barber is going to call Mrs. Marshall. She'll have a meal ready for us when we get home."

Bert thought he was going to starve before they reached the Marshall ranch. However, when they finally made it, he was glad they had waited. Mrs. Marshall had the table loaded with food, and there was indeed an apple pie for dessert.

"How did Bill Stewart ever get in with a gang like that?" Mrs. Marshall asked after she heard the account of the capture of the rustlers.

"Sheriff Cameron had suspected him for some time," Gramp answered. "I think Bill had been coaxed into some crooked gambling games and had lost so much to the rustlers that he was afraid to refuse to do what they wanted."

"We'll leave the trout with you, Mrs. Marshall," Gramp said as he and Bert got up to go. "We'll make another trip to Winding Creek before school starts. When we go we'll fish all the time. We won't have to look for rustlers."

Bert and his grandfather slept late next morning. They were finishing their breakfast when Spot gave the short, sharp bark he always did to announce the arrival of company. It was a familiar car that drove into the yard. Besides

117

the sheriff, Nancy, Jim, Mr. Marshall, and Mr. Henderson got out.

"We have recovered most of the stolen cattle," the sheriff announced. "All of yours are safe."

"They look funny with the Box B instead of your B over Bar brand," Jim said.

"They'll look good to me with any brand," Gramp told him. "I certainly couldn't afford to lose that many yearlings."

"You and Bert did your part toward getting them back," the sheriff assured him. "I've called the brand inspector. He'll be here later to straighten out the matter of the brands."

"Will the rest of you excuse me for a minute?" Gramp asked. "There's something I want to tell the sheriff and Bert."

The others nodded and moved out of hearing.

"I know I made a mistake when I didn't tell you where I got the money to pay off that loan, Walt," he said, "and I certainly should have told you, Bert."

"Forget it," the sheriff answered. "I knew you had a good reason for not telling me."

"A fellow who had owed me that much for a long time paid me unexpectedly," Gramp went on. "I could just as well have told you when you asked."

"Thanks for telling me now," Sheriff Cameron said. "Let's join the others. Mr. Henderson is anxious to make his announcement."

"The Ranchers' Protective Association gives a reward of one hundred dollars for information leading to the arrest of a rustler," Mr. Henderson told them. "We had a special meeting this morning and decided to pay you for each of the four rustlers. We thought Spot deserved a share, but a dog doesn't have much use for money. I have here a check for a hundred dollars for each of you."

"Wow!" Bert exclaimed. "A hundred dollars will outfit me for high school this fall."

"I'm glad we helped catch all but Bill," Nancy said as she accepted her check. "I wish we hadn't had to help catch him. He doesn't seem like a rustler."

"He was forced to join the gang because he owed Curly a gambling debt," Mr. Henderson explained. "He will have to be punished with the others. However, I'm sure he has learned his lesson and I'm going to give him his job back when he gets out of prison; that is, if the neighbors don't object."

"Nancy is sure Bill intended to protect her if it came to a showdown with Curly," Mr. Marshall said. "I want him to have another chance."

"So do I," Gramp agreed.

"That's settled then," Mr. Henderson was pleased. "And now to settle another matter. Spot dug a good gash in Curly's leg, but the doc sewed it up and there'll be no permanent damage." He smiled at Bert. "You don't have to worry about anyone taking a shot at your dog no matter where he goes. I told the Ranchers' Protective Association that anyone harming or trying to harm Spot would answer to me personally."

Spot realized he was being talked about. He sailed over the fence and trotted to Bert's side. He stood there wagging his tail and looking up at Mr. Henderson.

Jim walked over to stand beside Bert. He put one hand on Bert's shoulder and the other on Spot's head.

"You have quite a problem, Mr. Weston," he said with

a broad grin. "It isn't often that a rancher has to choose between a dog and a man to decide who's to be his top hand."

There was an answering smile on Gramp's face, but there was no mistaking the pride in his voice as he answered. "Either one is capable," he agreed. "But since Bert is still training Spot, I guess he'll be top hand and Spot will be his assistant."